One for sorrow, two for joy,
Three for a girl, four for a boy,
Five for silver, six for gold,
Seven for a secret never to be told,
Eight for a wish, **nine for a kiss** . . .

for a Kiss

Jenny Oldfield

Hodder
Children's
Books

a division of Hodder Headline

1

We're living through a heatwave. It's too much. Anyone with half a brain gets out of the city in summer.

That's what Kate did.

'Bye, Carter – have fun!' she told me, before she boarded the plane to spend July with her mom in Manhattan.

Melissa Brennan suddenly rediscovered her maternal instinct, said she wanted to spend time with her daughter. But I suspect it's more a case of Melissa wanting to get back together with Sean.

Concentrate, because this part is complicated. Kate's parents are divorced; Kate lives with Sean here in Fortune City, but right now he's working on an Angelworks project in New York. So, for Melissa to maximise the amount of time she spends with Sean, it helps to have Kate there too, to build bridges between them.

Get it? This makes Melissa look pretty manipulative, I know. Anyhow, the result is that Kate is currently starstruck in Manhattan and I'm sweating it out alone *chez* boring *moi*.

In two weeks I've received one wish-you-were-here postcard showing the art deco interior of the Chrysler Building, plus one short e-mail.

To: Joey C
From: Kbrennan@aol.com
Hi, Joey. It's hot. Dad and Angel are making a documentary on drop-dead gorgeous movie actor, Matt Kemp. I met him twice already. Problem – Matt *knows* he's drop-dead gorgeous. He has an ego the size of Everest. How are things with you? Catch up later.

I deleted the message – *zap!* I mean, I know who Matt Kemp is, for Chrissake! And what's new about a movie actor behaving like God? Then, since the e-mail, nothing.

'So, Carter . . .' Connie smiled at me in a certain way. Flirt alert!

That smile, the fact that we were hanging back behind Zig and Zoey as they walked arm-in-arm down Ginsberg Street towards the Lee Ahlberg actors' workshop.

I did my best to shrug the smile off and ignore Connie's pregnant pause. I mean, even I can recognise a play as obvious as the one Connie was making towards me.

'You heard from Kate lately?' She dropped the question

smooth as a round pebble in a pond. A thousand ripples ruffled the surface.

Silence from my end. Jeez, it was hot.

Connie never could take a hint. 'I talked with her on the phone this morning. She called me from New York. Sounds like she's having a great time.'

Thanks, Connie. Like, I really needed to know that.

'She's partying like crazy, surviving on four hours sleep per night. And she already met all the big names.'

I kicked an empty Coke can off the sidewalk and watched it roll into the gutter. If you read between the lines, you can see that I'm silently ripped apart by jealousy, and that Connie's tactic is to send me the strong message that since Kate clearly isn't interested in furthering our stagnating relationship, then how about her and me getting it together, baby?

I guess it was down to me for accepting Connie's invitation to attend the weekend theatre workshop with her in the first place.

'Show up for the opening session, see what you get out of it,' she'd suggested. 'There'll be a heap of kids you already hang out with there, and who knows, you may have a hidden talent!'

'Yeah, like Joey's the next Leonardo di Caprio!' Zig had sniggered.

Same as me, Zig had no interest in theatre, but Zoey

managed to drag him along anyway.

I only said yes because Zig had been too weak to say no to Zoey, and me, I'm just plain pathetic.

So here we were, Zig wishing he was tossing a ball into a basket, and me regretting that I'd given Connie an in.

'I got the low-down on Matt Kemp,' she confided.

How low down? Like, in how much detail? In my overheated imagination I pictured Kate scoring Matt Kemp's kisses out of ten for Connie's benefit.

'He has all these women throwing themselves at him.' I got the full picture from her. 'They hang around the film set and break into his hotel room at night. He never steps out of his door without a thousand photographers pointing their lenses in his face. But like, Kate's attitude is, "That don't impress me much!" With her dad working for Angel Christian all these years, she's been there, done that. Fame doesn't work any magic on Kate, you know, Carter.'

At last she had to stop and take a breath. I kicked another piece of garbage along the sidewalk.

'Hey!' Zoey turned with a yelp when the half-full OJ carton splashed against her bare heel and saturated her rope sandals.

'Yeah!' Connie walked on beside me, letting me fester. 'Between you and me, Joey, I get the feeling Kate has a fixation with Matt Kemp. She won't admit it because it wouldn't look cool, but she didn't stop talking about him all the time we were on the phone.'

We reached the entrance to the Ahlberg Centre just at the point where Zoey was having a problem getting Zig through the door.

'I'm really not comfortable with this,' he protested. For Zig, this was a long sentence.

'Jeez, Ziggy, cut it out.' Zoey grabbed him by the arm. He's six-two and she's five-four, so it looked kinda funny. 'Take Carter; he's not making any problems over this. I mean, you don't have to do a song and dance act in here. We already figured out that you're not John Travolta.'

'Will they make me act?' he whimpered.

Connie lost patience with him. 'Oh, Ziggy, leave it out! Work the lights, do the sound, make the coffee. Do anything you like, only stop blocking the doorway!'

I know about stage lights. That's my thing. To use Ziggy's phrase: I'm comfortable with that.

Connie's the big prima donna. Give her a stage and she'll take the centre. Ask her to cry on cue and she doesn't need an onion.

Don't get me wrong; I admire the talent, but at the same time I think it's weird when people hog the limelight. Personally I'd rather die than show myself up.

But hey, you know this already from when Kate and I worked the sound and the lights for the school production of *Death of a Salesman*.

Connie was developing some piece of method acting with a half-Chinese kid who lived a block down the street from me in Marytown. It involved a whole lot of grunting and long silences; difficult stuff for a girl like Connie to achieve.

An instructor was coaching them in the techniques, then moving on among other wannabe Brad Pitts and Jennifer Anistons. Meanwhile, Zig and I buried our heads in the Sport pages of the *Fortune City Times*.

Once, Zig looked up from the basketball scores to see the acting coach in a serious clinch with Zoey.

'Who *is* that guy?' he muttered.

I reached out across the lighting console to read a booklet of information about the workshops. 'That must be Johnny Hudson,' I informed him. 'He's a professional actor and session musician, as well as a part-time method-acting coach at West Beck Theatre School.'

'Does he have to enjoy his work so much?' Zig spoke through gritted teeth as Johnny embraced his girlfriend.

I grinned. 'What you gonna do; sock him in the jaw?'

Hudson was about as tall as Ziggy, with more bulk. He had biceps, and a six-pack so well defined you could see it clean through his white T-shirt.

Ziggy frowned. 'If you want my opinion, this acting stuff sucks!'

Yeah, I had to agree. Take Matt Kemp, the ego-mountain. Which started me thinking about Kate again. I mean, AGAIN. I was growing obsessive, in case you hadn't noticed.

Right this second Kate was most likely cruising around Manhattan in some movie star's red convertible. Or she was on the film set, sitting in Matt's canvas chair with his name stencilled on the back. He was leaning over her shoulder, explaining exactly why the lighting technician was using that particular filter for the shot they were setting up . . .

'Hey.' A girl sat on the stool beside me, resting her elbows on the edge of the lighting console.

First impression: wow!

'Hey,' I said back. Great conversationalist, that's me.

'I'm Beth Harvey.'

'Joey Carter.'

Wow, wow and mega-wow! Yeah, real juvenile, I admit. You want more specifics? Beth Harvey wore her blonde hair in a short, ragged cut. Spikes of the stuff fell forward over her pale forehead. She had the highest pair of cheekbones I've ever seen, the greenest eyes, the fullest mouth . . . Pause for breath. And she was looking at *me*. So I guess Kate wasn't the only one making new friends.

'What d'you do, Joey?' (Deep voice with a husky edge. Wow.)

'I'm still in High School.' Excellent, Carter!

'Oh really? I dropped out of college last fall,' Beth confided in me. She toyed with a lighting switch with the end of a long, blue-painted fingernail. 'West Beck; it's a good school, but I decided I needed more time to pursue my career.'

'So whad' youdo?' I gabbled.

'I'm an actress and a singer.'

'Are you famous?' Zig cut in with his usual finesse. 'Did you do a TV advert, did you get a hit single?'

Beth laughed out loud – beautiful *and* a sense of humour! 'I sing a kind of mixture of blues-rock; the sort of stuff you hear in clubs that doesn't make it into the charts. And no, I'm afraid I never did a TV ad.'

Zig temporarily lost interest and went back to the baseball reports.

'My sister is a rock star,' I boasted. Like, what was going on? I never normally used Marcie's super-stardom to enhance my own image. I must really have wanted to impress. 'She sings in a band called Synergie. You know her?'

'Sure. She has a great voice. How about you, Joey? Do you sing?'

'Only in the shower,' I leered. I mean; really!

Surprisingly, Beth didn't seem deterred by my cheesiness. 'So, do you act?'

'He acts *up*,' my friend Ziggy joked. 'Carter's always knee-deep in trouble.'

Beth raised a pale, slim, arched eyebrow. (I was paying her a lot of attention right then.) 'They call you Carter, do they?'

I nodded.

She nodded back. 'That fits. You're more of a Carter than a Joey.'

'So what are you doing here?' I lunged on, my heart thumping at the suspicion that a soulful, sensitive, talented and beautiful girl had just paid me a compliment – I think.

'I'm teaching singing to some of the younger kids as soon as they come out of dance class.'

By the way, Beth wore a skin-tight, strappy black top over loose, bright green, silk harem pants. That's the only way I can describe them. There was a gap between the short top and the low trousers and a silver stud glinting in her belly-button.

'What are you doing after the workshop?' she asked me.

Was I hallucinating, or had Beth Harvey just asked me what I was doing after the workshop?

Zig looked up from his newspaper with his jaw

hanging open. So yes, I'd heard her right.

'Erm – er – I – er, well.' Just let's say I was speechless too.

'Meet me in the plaza outside the main entrance?' Beth suggested. There was laughter again in her green eyes. Feline; yeah, that was the name for her eyes.

'You bet,' I gulped. Like John Boy in 'The Waltons'. Think of freckles and farm-dungarees, the IQ of a squid, the sophistication of a well-dressed amoeba.

It was still so hot after the class that I could feel small beads of perspiration standing out along my upper lip. I leaned against the doorway while small kids sprinted out and across the plaza to their moms and nannies sweltering inside their parked-up sports-utility vehicles.

'Coming, Joey?' Connie demanded. She'd emerged with Zoey and Zig and seen me lounging nonchalantly. 'We're planning a pizza-to-go, then heading back to my place for the evening.'

'No thanks.' I shrugged and kept a close lookout for Beth.

Now Beth and Connie look a little alike, as it happens. It's the halo of blonde hair that does it. And an in-your-face style.

But personality-wise, going on my first impression, I would put them pretty far apart. Connie is loud, whereas to me Beth seemed gentle and quiet. Connie has feminist opinions which she communicates strongly. Beth gave the impression that singing and acting were what mattered to her, but she would hang loose about everything else.

Oh, and major difference: whereas Connie was definitely a girls' type of girl (sisters under the skin, equality, sharing, support), Beth's style was definitely designed to attract the guys.

In fact, I would bet a lot of dough that most of Beth's friends were male.

'Whad'you mean, "No thanks"?' Connie echoed now. Like, I'd committed a capital offence. 'I said we're going over to my place.'

I shrugged and kept an eagle eye out for Beth.

'You're meeting that little singer woman!' Connie declared in an instant. Unerring instinct, I guess they call it. 'The one you couldn't take your eyes off!'

'So?' I didn't deny it. In any case, right that moment Beth was heading towards me across the entrance lobby of the Ahlberg building.

'So, how about tomorrow, Joey?' Con said in her loudest voice and manner. 'D'you plan to show up for more workshops?'

Beth slid alongside me and smiled up into my face.

My mumbled answer was that yeah, I guessed I would

11

put in an appearance. Frankly, my mind was welded to the fact that Beth had just slipped an arm round my waist. It was like an electric current shooting through me.

'So I can tell Kate that you're a wannabe Matt Kemp?' Connie goaded. Jeez, there were daggers in her eyes.

'Matt who?' I countered with a neat put-down.

'Oh, very funny, Joey.' By this time, Connie couldn't hide her contempt. 'So I can talk with Kate and say you suddenly developed an interest in theatre work?'

I could see Beth thinking, 'Kate who?', just like Connie intended. But her arm slid further round my waist, and her fingers hooked into the belt loop of my jeans.

'Say it's the computerised lighting system that turns me on.' I gave Connie a fake grin and rested my arm round Beth's shoulder. Wow, was this weird. As soon as Kate was off the scene, I had women fighting over me. I mean, Joey Carter, Joe Public, boring *moi*?

'Whatever.' Connie's dagger-stare fixed itself on Beth. But her dignity wouldn't allow her to let rip directly. She just glared at her rival, assessing the similar haircut, the high cheekbones and the green eyes to check out whether or not Beth was wearing coloured lenses.

'Jeez, I need to eat!' Ziggy groaned from somewhere on the sidelines.

By this time, the centre was practically empty. I spotted

the last kids trail out of the door, followed by the drama coach, Johnny Hudson.

'Gimme pizza!' Zig moaned. 'Feed me, feed me!'

'Let's go,' Zoey threw in. Behind Connie's back, she gave me a small, 'go for it' smile which I ignored.

Anyhow, Johnny Hudson evidently wanted us to move on. By this time he'd locked the double doors and set the security system. He clocked Beth standing with me, did a serious double-take (like, did I have six arms and alien antennae sticking out the top of my head, or something?), then hustled us all out into the plaza.

'See ya, Joey,' Zig said, happy to amble off in search of a four-cheeses, deep-pan special.

And that was how come Beth Harvey and I strolled home together in the warm evening shadows.

When I say 'home', I mean her place, which was ten storeys up in an old tenement in East Village. So we had to stroll arm-in-arm down Ginsberg Street, take a left on to Rothko Square, cut across on a diagonal and hit the subway under East Grand Street.

This is the area of Fortune City where the college students hang out; they sit in the street cafés reading thick books, looking cool in places named after famous American writers and artists. Like, drinking cappuccino in a bar called Kerouac's improves your IQ. Not.

In East Village you find mainly wannabes walking the tree-lined streets and chilling out in the tiny parks.

So Beth and I were using the subway, and she was saying she'd be real happy for me to walk her all the way home.

'This subway makes me nervous,' she admitted. And her arm round my waist did tense a little as she passed the remark.

To me it felt ordinary: concrete walls, graffiti, an unpleasant smell. But not in any way spooky. And in any case, at eight-thirty in the evening, it was still broad daylight.

We breathed easier as we came up the far side and took the nearest left down a narrow alleyway between blocks.

Beth's block faced on to Franklin Avenue, but her tenth-storey apartment was most easily reached by a metal fire escape down the side of the building. The alleyway was deep in shadow when we arrived, partly blocked by giant trash cans and by a monster Harley Davidson motorcycle. For some reason, the gleaming machine worried her.

'Wait!' she muttered, stepping back behind a metal trash can and pulling me with her.

We held back a minute or two before the bike rider came down the fire escape taking the metal stairs two at a time. He wore a black helmet with the visor down, black leather pants and an unzipped, matching jacket. My glimpse of the guy gave the impression of a young, tall, well-made individual who worked out at the gym.

Beth saw him and pressed herself hard against the brick wall. She waited until she heard the roar of the Harley engine and saw the bike and rider exit the alley. Then she pushed herself free of the wall and leaned against me.

She was trembling pretty hard, I can tell you.

So I had to help her up the ten flights of steps. 'Who was that guy on the bike?' I asked.

Beth shook her head. 'I don't know.'

'Have you seen him before? Does he live in the building?'

Same answer: 'Don't know.' Which answered the second question, but didn't tell me whether or not she had seen him before.

'So, what's the problem?' I asked, as we reached her landing.

She was panting a little from the climb. That husky voice was breathless as she forced a smile. 'No problem, Carter; really!'

So why the hide-and-seek behind the trash can?

And why the rose carefully laid along the peeling window ledge?

It was one of those perfect specimens: a single stem, a

few thorns, glossy green leaves. And half-opened, deep crimson, velvety petals.

Beth spotted it and froze.

'Looks like you have an admirer,' I said. You can rely on me to say the obvious.

She let out a sharp burst of breath, dived forward, took a hold of the rose by the head and crushed its soft petals between her fingers.

Then she flung the whole thing over the rail of the fire escape.

Last thing I saw, the stem was plummeting to the ground, the blood-red petals fluttering more slowly and delicately after it.

2

Sometimes I think I must be dreaming.

It's summer and New York is too hot to bear, so everyone exits over the Brooklyn Bridge and heads downstate for the Hamptons. Picture an open-top convertible, the wind in your hair, the sad Statue of Liberty waving goodbye.

Then I open my eyes and I, Kate Brennan, am truly sitting next to Matt Kemp, film-star, who has invited me out to his friend's place for the weekend.

His co-star, Kris Moss, and his director, Val Cominesci, will also be there, along with Honor-Lee Matthews, the rising star in the Movieworld galaxy.

Oh, and my dad, Sean Brennan, with his boss, Angel Christian. This may cramp my style, I admit. But then, Dad and Angel will be busy with work most of the time. They're already behind schedule with the documentary they're making about Matt, so Angel will be in frenetic mode, interviewing anything that moves.

However, my mom has also threatened to show up

in West Hampton, under the pretext of being my chaperone, but really because this glitzy partying stuff is just her scene.

Come Monday, back at her art gallery in Manhattan, she'll be doing some serious name-dropping. 'As I was saying to my friend, Val – Val Cominesci; you know, the famous Eastern European movie director . . .' Or, 'Honor-Lee Matthews is such a sweet girl. You know she just went through a bad break-up with her boyfriend, Kris Moss? And the two of them still have to work on Val's movie for another whole month. God knows how the poor kid will keep her head together for that length of time!'

I've warned Matt about Mom, and he says, 'No problem. If she gives us any trouble, I'll set my security gorillas loose!'

I laugh and tell him no security guy on this planet could prove a match for my mom.

We were sweeping out along the coast road when I told him this.

The houses facing on to the beach were inhabited by legends of the movie and music industry. They could wake up every morning to the sound of the Atlantic Ocean crashing on to the shore and the roar of earth-diggers moving in next door. The new owners would plan to demolish last year's star's place because it wasn't elegant enough. Not enough sauna-rooms, a too-small gymnasium, and only ten underground car-parking spaces for guests.

'That's what I like about you, Kate Brennan,' Matt replied. He was wearing shades so I couldn't read his expression. 'You refuse to be impressed.'

'What did you expect?' I pushed my hair back from my face, leaned out of the car and enjoyed the view of the coastline.

'Adulation.' Matt swung the convertible off the main route and took a side road leading to the sea. 'Adoration. Fixation. The stuff I always get.'

I grinned. 'Since when?'

'Since I was a kid in high school.'

'Before you were famous?'

'Sure. I was always the most popular guy around.'

'With the biggest ego.' Now I was really laughing out loud. 'What must it be like being born with those fabulous good looks, that impressive physique?'

Matt released the wheel, raised his sunglasses and shot me a glance. '*You* tell ME.'

'Hah!' I blushed in case he thought I'd set myself up for this shallow compliment. I hadn't. 'Keep a hold of the steering-wheel, for Chrissakes!'

The car swerved into some gravel at the side of the

winding road, its rear wheels spun, then Matt pulled it back on track.

So I'd better say something about the looks and the physique. Matt's, I mean.

He has a small nose and rounded mouth, with heavy, dark eyebrows over clear blue eyes. That's the killer combination: dark complexion and eyes the colour of the ocean under an azure sky.

I guess the overall impression of Matt's face is moody. The natural set for his mouth is down at the corners; he has a slight, guarded frown creasing his forehead. But the blue eyes invite a girl to find the key to unlock that suspicious frown, and when he unexpectedly turns on the smile, it can come with all the force of a space launch at Cape Kennedy. *Three-two-one . . . lift-off!*

This combined with broad shoulders, slim waist, good butt and long legs is enough to explain why Matt Kemp is one of the hottest properties in Hollywood, and why Angel Christian considers him interesting enough to make a documentary about.

Oh, and why I was sitting in the passenger seat of his red convertible.

I admit it, I was swept off my feet by the partying, the car, the big money, plus the face and the physique. I'm not proud of it. But try telling me honestly that you'd do it any differently.

OK, so back home there was Carter. A million miles away, in a different lifetime, maybe there had been something between us. With Joey it was always difficult to tell.

He's not exactly open with his emotions. I give him chances which he fails to take. In the end, I have to think that maybe he just isn't interested.

I put this depressing possibility to Connie Oseles only last night. She'd called me from Fortune City for all the movie star gossip. Had Kris Moss really split with Honor-Lee, or was that just a cheap journalistic shot? Was Honor-Lee actually the daughter of a Cree Native American, or were her ancestors French Canadian trappers? I eventually turned the conversation around towards Carter, via Ziggy and Zoey.

'How's Joey doing?' I asked.

'You know Carter. The same.' Connie gave me zilch information.

'Is he still stacking supermarket shelves?'

'No, he quit. Hey, he decided to come to a theatre workshop this weekend – surprise, huh?'

'Carter did?'

'Yeah. We'll have fun. Hey, did you really get this invite to spend time with Matt Kemp?'

'Yeah, I did. Connie, I need to know: does Carter ever – well, does he – I mean . . .'

'. . . Ever talk about you, Kate?' She paused to think. 'Nope, sorry. But hey, don't read too much into that. You know Carter . . .'

My heart sank as she trailed off with this feeble attempt to keep up my spirits.

We signed off after what felt to me like a significant conversation. I put down the phone. So Carter didn't care. Absence didn't make the heart grow fonder, except inside the covers of a slushy romance.

The narrow, twisting track which Matt had taken led us down to the place we were staying. I won't go into too much detail; just to say it was the size of a hotel in a garden as big, green and smooth as a golfing fairway. You could invite twenty guests here for the weekend, and the house would still seem under-occupied.

Matt parked the car outside the main entrance and vaulted out. I chose the slower and more conventional method of opening the door and stepping on to the driveway. The sun burned through my thin, white cotton shirt, though a fresh breeze off the ocean went a little way to making the heat bearable.

'Party time!' Matt said brightly. He'd noticed the distant throb of music playing through speakers on the beach, so he took me by the hand and we scooted round the side of the house to a wide expanse of sand in a pretty bay bordered by cliffs and trees. No other houses; remember, this was a private beach belonging to one very rich person.

Though it was only 7.30 p.m., the party was already happening. People were dancing in the sand, then running into the shallow waves to get their expensive clothes all wet. Somebody suggested stripping off clothes to take a proper swim, which prompted a heated debate about tides and currents and talk of a minor celebrity who once drowned in the sea while smashed on cocaine.

So no swimming. Just plenty of sea-food to eat and alcohol to drink, and loud, loud music.

'They're playing Synergie's new album!' I yelled at Matt above the noise. I told him that I knew the lead singer, Marcie Carter's brother, Joey.

Marcie's voice rose and soared like a bird over the water.

'It's a mystery to me,
Mystery to me.
Won't you ever see
Love will always be
A mystery to me . . .'

Upbeat, pumping out the lyrics to a dance rhythm, then dropping to a slow, lingering beat when you realise the magical mystery of love has turned to pain and confusion.

Matt looped an arm round my shoulder and took me into the crowd.

Some guys I already knew. Kris and Honor-Lee were both there and making a big show of blanking the other out. Angel had showed up with a film crew, but as yet I saw no sign of my dad, her producer. Then I did spot him, sitting on a rock with his bare feet dangling in the water, deep in conversation with the director, Val Cominesci. When he saw me arrive with Matt, he gave an understated wave, then carried on talking movies with Val.

Not so Mommy dearest. The moment she saw me walk in with Matt she split from her group and zoomed in like an Exocet missile.

'Hey, Kate, hey, Matt!' she cooed across the warm sand, as if every day her sixteen–year-old daughter walked in with the world's hottest young movie actor.

'Mom,' I acknowledged in a tone intended to make her butt out.

Having a mom like mine is tough. Besides being the pushiest person on the planet, she also looks young enough to be my big sister. She works at it with the creams and the lotions, the exercise machines and the personal trainer, and she sure gets a terrific result. Eat your heart out every other forty year old in New York.

'No, really!' Matt looked from me to Mom and came on with the schmooze. 'You can't be . . . no, it's impossible!'

Mom made simpering noises of protest, then accepted the compliment. 'I thought you were terrific in "Moonwalk",' she flattered him back.

'Yeah? You've no idea how hot I got inside that spacesuit. I lost thirteen pounds in weight.' As Matt slid easily into talking through his greatest acting roles with Mom, I took a look around.

I noticed Angel, dressed in a shapely pink basque number over straight white pants, cleverly corner Honor-Lee for an off-the-record heart to heart which would duly figure prominently in the documentary on Matt. Glossy little pink Angel didn't know the meaning of the word confidential.

Long-limbed, lethargic, pale and beautiful Honor-Lee, with the dead straight, jet-black hair of the Cree Native American, fell all too easily into Angel's honey trap. She would spill her guts at this beach party and have to run crying to her libel lawyer to limit the damage she'd allowed the high-profile television documentary maker to inflict.

'There's a question in my mind,
Question in my mind.
Please don't make me find
Your answer is unkind
To the question in my mind . . .'

Marcie Carter's voice sang on above the smack of the waves against the cliffs and the rippling chatter of the party guests.

'Kate, honey; come over with me to meet Val.' It looked like Mom had come on with the flattery too heavily even for the mega-star. He gave me a shrug and sidled away, giving her the space to step in and guide me by the elbow.

'I already met Val on set,' I objected.

Mom paid no attention. 'I just had this long, fascinating talk with him about the political content of Eastern European movies. I mean, really in-depth discussion.'

She propelled me across the soft sand to the rocks where Dad and Val sat. Meanwhile, Matt had been absorbed by a crowd of fellow actors and wannabes.

'Gee, Matt is cute!' Mom hissed in transit to meet

her famous new friend. 'I mean, in person, he's the sort of guy you just want to eat!'

'Mom!'

'It's OK, he can't hear me.'

'Cut it out anyway, OK!'

The grip on my elbow tightened. 'You know your problem, Kate? You don't realise how up-front you need to be with a guy like Matt Kemp. I mean, he has a hundred women falling at his feet every day of his life, so there's no point in you playing it shy and sensitive.'

By this time, we'd reached Dad and Val, so I took a deep breath and said nothing. And I tried not to react to the comedy show Mom put on, flirting like crazy with Val Cominesci, doing the intellectual bit to impress him, and all for Dad's benefit.

I guess Val didn't know Mom and Dad's history. All he saw was a good-looking, sophisticated woman making a play for him. She talked French movies, German movies, art-house movies and the place of cinema in the twenty-first century; the poor guy never stood a chance.

'What an amazing woman!' he said in his thick accent as Mom took a break from impressing him for a quick bitching session with Angel. 'And really beautiful.'

'But she snores in her sleep,' Dad said quietly.

End of conversation.

Val went mumbling and stumbling away to join another group.

I grinned at Dad.

'You doing OK?' he murmured.

'Yeah, excellent. I came with Matt Kemp.'

'I know you did. That's why I asked.'

'Dad, I can take care of myself . . .' I began.

'Just take it easy,' he warned, before Mom showed up again at his shoulder.

'Take no notice of your father,' she interrupted. 'He's out of touch with young people. I say, go ahead and have a good time. It's not every girl who gets the chance to date a drop-dead gorgeous movie actor.'

'Yeah.' I could see him now, prising himself out of his group of hangers-on and making his way back towards me. 'I guess he *is* good-looking.'

'Mystery to me, Mystery to me . . .' Marcie's song faded and died.

I definitely felt a certain physical chemistry going on between me and the beautiful Matt as he approached.

Mom laughed and repeated to him exactly what I'd said and the laid-back way I'd said it.

Matt grinned. His blue eyes gazed right into mine. 'You wanna dance to this next song?'

I nodded and kicked off my shoes.

Dancing in fine, warm sand is weird. More of a shuffle really. And the number was slow; the type you get into a clinch for. It was growing dusk, the sun was fading, the sky washed with a golden-pink glow.

'OK?' Matt whispered in my ear.

I nodded, then rested my head against his shoulder.

His arms tightened around the back of my waist. 'Romantic, huh?'

Another nod. My heart was beating louder than the drum on the track that was playing.

We drifted in tight, slow circles, further and further away from the other dancers.

'I'm light-headed,' I murmured as the world began to spin. There was silver sea, white waves, dark sand, pink and golden sky all spinning around me.

'Must be love,' Matt whispered back. His lips touched my neck.

More spinning and turning, heart thumping like crazy.

A kiss on my neck, my chin, my lips.

A kiss.

I lost it and kissed him back.

The name, the face, the lips inside my head as I closed my eyes weren't Matt Kemp's. And the troubled grey eyes that stared deep into my guilty heart and soul belonged to far-off Joey Carter.

3

I read it on my e-mail before I saw it in the newspapers. 'Matt Kemp Dates Sixteen-year-old Nymphet – Official!'

Kate wrote me on-line two days before the story broke, which was a week after she'd attended the house party in West Hampton.

To: Joey C
From: Kbrennan@aol.com
Hey. Sorry I haven't been in touch. Heaps of stuff happening here, most of which probably wouldn't interest you. I mean, there's not a big ball game in sight. Just boring movie stars.

Which is why I'm contacting you now. You'll read it in the newspapers pretty soon, so I wanted to tell you face to face (monitor to monitor), that I'm seeing Matt Kemp.

I know; I'm in shock too.

It all fell together real fast – don't ask me how. Matt's warned me that the press will get a hold of it. Like, it's front page news when he gets a new haircut, let alone a new girlfriend.

Mom's already taken me down Fifth Avenue on a shopping splurge, in preparation for the camera lights to start flashing. Typical, huh?

So, Carter, that's my news.

I spoke to Connie and she tells me you started seeing some singer called Beth. Good luck with that.

Way to go, Joey. See ya.

I was reading between the lines of this, driving myself crazy, when Fern, my kid sister crept into my room. She snuggled up beside me as I stared at the screen.

She wanted to read the message on screen. I shook my head. 'Later,' I told her.

This kid is only nine and she can't speak or hear well. But she picks up how a person's feeling and tunes in big time. She knew the e-mail had made me sad – worse, actually. I was totally gutted.

Kate, didn't you know the way I felt about you? Did I need to spell it out? I thought we had something good building – a slow burn. A communication that couldn't be hurried or squeezed out of shape into some boring dating arrangement. I mean, it never felt right to flirt with you, or come on heavy. There were times I wanted to make a move . . . yeah, lots of times.

Fern snuck close and gave me a hug. Don't be sad, Joey.

I read Kate's message a dozen times, looking for a hint, a way of e-mailing her back to tell her how I really felt. But no, it was too late. She'd moved on, and in a big way. I mean, how did I even begin to compete with a movie star?

Kate, I don't blame you. If I'd been you, I'd have moved on too. It's me; I'm a schmuck who's too screwed up to show his real feelings. I missed my chance. Story of my life.

Fern squeezed and squeezed me, her skinny arms round me, her dark brown eyes filling up and brimming over.

I hugged her back. The weird thing was, there were tears in my eyes too.

'So how come you don't leave the house these days?'

My big sister, Marcie, had picked up on the fact that my social life was virtually extinct.

That was probably down to my mom. 'Joey just stays in his room, moping over Kate,' she would tell Marcie. 'Ever since that picture appeared in the newspapers of her and Matt Kemp at a party in West Hampton, your brother stopped going anywhere, doing anything. Even Ziggy can't get him out of the house to watch the ball game!'

The two of them, Mom and Marcie, would chew over the problem whenever they talked on the phone. Then

Marcie got back from touring with the band and gave me a hard time. Like now.

'Joey, what happened between you and Kate?'

'Big round zero.' *Butt out!* I warned with my body language. In other words, I was horizontal in front of the TV, not even glancing at Marcie.

She flicked it off with the remote. 'OK, so you and Kate are history. That's a pity. I like Kate. But it doesn't mean the end of life as we know it.'

Silence from me. I still stared at the blank screen. I could see my sullen reflection in the shiny grey square.

'So what about Connie Oseles?' Marcie persisted.

'What about Connie?'

'Mom said she called you two, three times a day all last week.'

'So?'

'OK, so Connie's not your type. But what about this Beth Harvey?'

I made the effort to prop myself upright on the sofa. 'Jeez, whose life is this anyway?'

'Yours, Joey. But Mom's uptight about you. She says Beth came round to the house a couple of days back, left you this ticket for the gig tonight, at the Lemon House.'

I noticed Marcie scoop up the square yellow card from the coffee table and read the details. In my own mind, I'd already decided that the music club where Beth was due to sing wasn't my scene. I planned an evening in watching sport.

'Hmm.' Marcie read carefully, took in the venue and date. She pulled me up on my feet. 'C'mon, Joey, grab a jacket!'

'Why? Where am I going?'

Marcie was hauling me across the room, scooping my jacket from off the floor, shoving it into my arms. She was small and slight, but determined. 'Lemon House,' she insisted. 'I'll call Ocean for him to meet us there. Synergie need extra backing singers for the next tour. Who knows; maybe Beth Harvey will turn out to be the girl we've been looking for!'

'I like this place, it's cool.'

Ocean removed his shades and took a look around the music club – small, intimate, with low lighting and not a citrus fruit in sight.

He liked it because the people there knew who he was, but didn't give him any hassle. Like, we know you're a brilliant rock guitarist, up there with the greats, but we respect your right to show up incognito at a small, East Village venue like Lemon House. We're cool dudes around here. So, no sweat.

Currently there was an unexciting blues band playing from a crowded platform. I also noted a bar in one corner and a haphazard arrangement of tables and seats. For a hot Thursday night in the middle of summer, the place was humming, mainly with college students and young professors.

'Where's Beth Harvey?' Marcie wanted to know the moment we walked in.

I'd already picked out her blonde hair, tight top made up of silver sequins and short black leather skirt. Likewise, she'd seen me. Her face lit up big-time as she headed across the crowded room.

'Hey, you made it!' Taking my hand, she kissed me on the cheek.

Marcie took note: the kiss, the clothes, the high-heeled ankle-boots.

'You're Joey's sister.' Beth took the lead in the conversation, unawed by the presence of two members of Synergie. In fact, Ocean and Marcie being there seemed to give her a definite buzz. It was like when you jerk the ring-pull of a can of Coke, and the whole thing froths out. 'Hey, it's fantastic that you came. You too, Ocean. Yeah. How long since Synergie did a gig in a place this size, huh?'

'It's cool,' Ocean insisted, settling down at the bar and ordering a drink, like he intended to make the most of the evening.

'When I gave Carter the ticket, I never imagined you

two would be in town!' Beth gushed.

Not quite true. I recalled a conversation with Beth about Synergie's schedule. She'd wanted to know when the band would next touch base here in Fortune City. In fact, she'd shown a strong interest in everything to do with my mega-successful sister. Well, she was in the same musical pond; a little fish to Marcie's monster marlin.

'But I'm so happy you came! Did Carter tell you about us – that we're an item?'

We were? OK, we were. What did I care?

Marcie blinked back her surprise. 'You know Joey,' she shrugged. 'You're lucky if he gives you the time of day.'

One kiss on a fire escape made us an item?

I guess I didn't mention the kiss.

This happened after Beth crushed the red rose and flung it over the rail. It was a fumbled type of thing: her taking me by surprise and me screwing up the opportunity to kiss her back. That's why I didn't dwell on it at the time.

Unlike Beth, who seemed to be reading the whole Romeo and Juliet thing into one messed-up moment. One kiss? Who made that rule?

I guess I didn't do as good a job of hiding my amazement as Marcie had. I mean, hadn't Beth noticed that I didn't return any of her calls after the fire escape incident, or that she'd had to call round to my house in person to drop off the Lemon House entry tickets?

'That looks like news to Joey!' Ocean laughed.

'Yeah, well, he's kinda shy,' Beth acknowledged.

'Plus, he has a girl in New York,' Marcie observed. She must have had a complex motive for saying this, since she already knew about Kate and the Matt Kemp thing.

'Oh, you mean Kate Brennan?' Beth came back fast and slick. 'Yeah, Connie Oseles mentioned her. But that's history, isn't it, Carter?'

I nodded. *Wow, that hurt.*

Luckily, this stuff was cut short by a signal from the guitarist on stage. It looked like it was Beth's cue to join them.

'Hey, I gotta go,' she announced. Then she sailed between the tables, up on to the platform, head held high, sashaying on her high-heels.

'Hmm,' was all Marcie said.

'Joey, man; it's your lucky night,' Ocean grinned.

Beth took the microphone. A million stage lights reflected in those tiny silver discs making up her strapless top. As the music began to drive and push to a soul beat, she stood square on the platform, feet apart, face expressionless. Then she opened her mouth and sang.

* * *

'Cool,' was Ocean's verdict.

Get this: the more famous you grow, the smaller your vocabulary becomes. Ocean used to be an English major in college in his previous life.

'She sings OK,' Marcie opined quietly, as the audience applauded Beth's first song.

'That's one in-your-face girl.' Ocean stuck with his high opinion of her style. 'She sings and she doesn't give a damn whether you like it or not. This is her voice, take it or leave it.'

Most people nearby were taking it. They were clapping loud for the husky, deadpan delivery.

'The weird thing is, she's not like that in real life,' I pointed out.

'Hmm.' Marcie's grunt contained doubt bordering on cynicism. Like, she'd jumped to certain unfavourable conclusions about Beth.

'No, really. She's not that confident. She freaks out when she walks under subways. She doesn't like walking home alone.'

'Hmm.'

'Jeez, Joey . . . Man, she's coming on strong!'

OK, so I was dumb. But I was pig-headed too. I insisted that Beth might have a reason to be nervous; namely the leather-clad guy with the Harley Davidson.

'Bad scene!' Marcie warned as Beth began her second

number. 'This guy on the motorcycle; does she know who he is?'

'No, but he leaves her flowers,' I told her. 'The way I look at it is that this guy has seen Beth sing or act. Maybe he's been to a theatre workshop; who knows? And he's developed this fantasy relationship with her, following her around, leaving her roses.'

' "Rose" or "roses"?' Marcie checked.

Ocean sat on his bar stool and swayed to the new, slow blues number, ignoring all this.

'Plural. Beth says it's reached the stage where she feels nauseous at the sight of any rose anywhere – in a florist's, growing in someone's garden. Apparently this guy has developed a total obsession.'

'Joey!' Marcie shook her head like I was a hopeless case. 'Watch what you're getting into here, OK!'

'You mean, you never had a fan sending you flowers?' I countered.

'Touché!' Ocean grunted, dredging a hard word from out of his memory bank. This guy writes the lyrics for all Synergie's songs, remember. 'Hey, you two, why don't you quit arguing and listen to this woman sing?'

I walked home with Beth after the Lemon House gig.

She'd been on a high ever since Ocean had offered her the chance to audition as a backing singer for the band, which he did immediately after she finished her set.

'I don't believe it!' she said over and over.

'You better.' The fresh night air bathed our faces after the sweaty fug of the club. We strolled along East Grand Street and took the subway, came up on Franklin Avenue. 'Beth, when a chance like this comes your way, you gotta grab it.'

'Oh sure, I'll show up for the audition, don't you worry.' Beth's step was bouncy past the graffiti, up the slope on to ground level. Car headlights raked the high walls of the tenements, swung round corners and glared in our faces until we turned down the side alley out of their way. 'Joey, this could be my big break. I'm so glad you persuaded Marcie and Ocean to come along tonight. I can't thank you enough!'

Whoa! This is the part where I should have explained to Beth that the Lemon House hadn't been my idea. But confessions are hard when a beautiful, talented girl a couple of years older than you stops you on the sidewalk and kisses you.

No fumbling this time. This occasion was lips on lips.

When she led me on up the fire escape to her apartment, my legs were weak at the knees. Literally.

'Come in for coffee,' Beth whispered, totally ignoring the red rose laid neatly across her doorstep.

* * *

Call me fickle. Call me what you like. Just put your hand on your heart and swear you wouldn't have done the same thing.

This was my first experience of being swept off my feet and I was gonna milk it.

I met Beth next morning for coffee in the Ahlberg Centre. I met her in the evening to catch a movie. Next day and the next we found a dozen good reasons to spend time together. Sunday evening, Beth was singing at the Lemon House again. Monday morning, she was due to audition for Ocean.

'Carter, come to the gig.' She called to invite me along.

'I'll try. Only, Mom asked me to babysit Fern and Damien for her tonight after they all get back from the theme park,' I said, still sounding like a hick country boy.

'Oh, Joey . . .' Beth's voice fell flat. 'Who's gonna walk me home after the gig?'

'OK, leave it with me.' Maybe I could ask Marcie to childmind instead of me. 'I'll move a few mountains and see you there.'

I received some phone kisses and a few whispers in my ear, then I finished the call to answer the doorbell.

'. . . Kate!' My jaw dropped and felt like it smashed to pieces on the doorstep.

'Hey, Carter.'

She looked tanned and uncertain, staring at me with her dark brown eyes.

'What happened?'

'What d'you mean, "what happened"? I flew back with Dad for a few days. He and Angel finished filming, so I came home with him.'

'Why didn't you call?'

'I did. You were out. Didn't Damien pass on the message?'

I shook my head, still barring Kate's way into the house with the half-closed door. 'Are you back in Fortune City for good?' (Which was thinly disguised code for asking if she and Matt Kemp were still an item.)

Kate's turn to shake her head. 'Joey, we need to talk.'

'What about?' I mean, what was there to talk about? She'd e-mailed me then fallen out of my stratosphere. These days I only saw her picture in magazines.

And it wasn't as if she even looked like the old Kate.

The Kate I knew wore casual clothes – trainers, loose trousers, sport tops. She let her long dark hair hang down and half hide her face, which generally didn't have any cosmetic help. This new one standing on my stoop wore her hair on top of her head and plenty of mascara. And there was nothing laid back or sporty about the slim cream shift dress she was wearing.

'Can I come in?'

'Sure.' I flipped the door open with my foot and made out like I didn't care whether she came in or not.

'How are you doin', Carter?' She looked around, saw the same old place – the kicked paintwork, the scuffed walls.

'Good.' Like, the new glitzy, glamorous Kate had flown hundreds of miles from Manhattan just to ask me how I was doing?

'Really?'

'Yeah, good.' Build a brick wall a hundred feet high, don't let her near me. 'I've been working quite a bit on the lighting system over at the Ahlberg Centre.'

'Yeah, Connie told me.' Kate's gaze rested on the baseball cap she'd once given to Fern as a gift. It was lying on the hall floor, all screwed up.

'How's Matt?' I asked, straight out.

She flinched. 'Matt's good. He flew to LA to see his agent. He'll be back in New York in a few days.'

After this, there was an awkward silence, the first I'd had with Kate. Ever, in my life.

And right after that, there was another ring on the bell.

I opened the door. '. . . Beth!' Didn't she hear me distinctly say that I'd see her at the Lemon House?

'Hey, Joey. I was two streets away when I called, so I came straight over . . .' Catching sight of Kate standing

43

in the hall, Beth's voice faltered. She looked at me like I'd killed my own grandmother.

'Beth, this is Kate. Kate . . . Beth.' I made the faltering introductions. This was unreal.

They stared and scored each other out of ten the way girls do. Like, life's a competition with strict rules and a row of judges inside their heads, holding up score cards: nine point five, nine-seven, full marks.

Kate's nerve was the first to break. 'I'm out of here,' she muttered.

I followed her out of the house on to the sidewalk. 'I thought you said you wanted to talk?'

'No, Carter, not now.' She glanced back at Beth with her rough cap of spiky blonde hair, standing in my doorway.

'I wasn't expecting . . . I mean, how was I . . . ?' Struggling to find a reason for Kate to change her mind and not walk out of my life for good, I came up with garbage. 'Look, call me tomorrow, OK!'

Kate's shrug indicated that no, she wouldn't bother to do that.

'Why not?' Jeez, my mind was imploding at the exact same time that my heart was trying to hammer its way through my ribcage.

Kate had Matt Kemp and I had Beth Harvey, that was why not.

'Call me,' I begged as she walked away.

She stopped for a split second and I thought she'd changed her mind. But then she shook her head and threw me a cutting jibe before she walked on down the street. 'Hey, Joey. Maybe we should set up a double date – you and Beth, me and Matt. Think about it!'

4

So, the summer sizzled on.

I really had it made: the guy, the fame, the money.

'Matt Kemp adores you, darling!' Mom was convinced that I was about to make a beautiful teenaged bride. She was already on the phone, trying to tempt me back to New York.

'Quit it, Mom. I don't need the pressure.'

'What pressure? I'm only stating the obvious: the man is crazy for you. Didn't you say he's called every night from LA since he flew out?'

First to New York, at my mom's place, and now back home in Fortune City, it was true that Matt was building up a giant phone bill. He told me how his agent was signing him up to a new movie deal worth millions of dollars. The filming was scheduled to begin almost as soon as his current movie in Manhattan was in the can. It would mean flying out to the mountains in Nepal, and Matt had already invited me along.

'We'll have a wild time,' he promised. 'No pressmen

hanging around, no crazy fans. Just you and me up a snowy mountain!'

The snowy mountain sounded good. I said I'd have to think it through.

'What's to think?' Matt pushed harder. 'Kate, I'm inviting you on a trip of a lifetime, so what's the problem?'

'School is the problem,' I pointed out. 'My fall semester coincides with this Nepal thing.'

Matt's solution was instant. 'So quit school.'

And this was the dilemma I was discussing with Mom now.

'Kate, honey, you simply can't turn down this chance.' A typical mom, she was one hundred and ten per cent in favour. 'School, college; all that stuff can wait. But let me tell you, you'll never get another opportunity to turn your life around the way you could with Matt.'

'What if Matt and I don't work out?' It still felt so weird dating him and having him call me. And, as you know, I couldn't get Carter out of my head.

'You *will* work out!' Mom insisted. Like, the idea of failure was blasphemy – against her religion. 'You two look great together!'

'OK, so I'm thinking about it.' I said this so I could end the conversation, aware that Dad was hovering in my bedroom doorway, waiting to speak with me.

'Well, move it,' was Mom's parting shot. 'Matt's the type of guy who could lose interest real fast.' *Bang*, the phone went down.

Thanks, Mom, for viewing him as ideal boyfriend material then.

I guess she meant well and wanted the best for me. Only her 'best' and mine didn't always match up.

'Problem?' Dad asked.

He'd been working Sunday and had just got back from editing the Matt Kemp programme in the Angelworks studio.

'That was Mom,' I sighed. I felt suddenly tired and low.

Dad came quietly into the room. 'So, tell me.'

'She wants me to quit school and take the trip with Matt.' I sat heavily on my bed, grabbed a pillow and squeezed it tight against my stomach.

'Yeah.' The news came as no surprise to Dad. He stood watching me, saying very little. 'How about you, Kate? What do *you* want?'

'I don't know. I'm pulled two ways. Maybe more.' I thought it was my stomach hurting, but when I hugged the pillow close, I found it was my heart. 'One; I think Nepal could be magic. Two; Nepal with Matt could also be fun. But three; Nepal with Matt and a whole film crew seems like less of a good time. I mean, I'd be sitting by myself on a snowy mountain formost of the day while they all work like crazy to meet deadlines. Four; I'd also kinda like to finish school and then decide what to do with the rest of my life.'

'Yeah,' Dad said. He kept on looking at me hard.

'Five; if I went with Matt I'd be real homesick thinking about you and Fortune City . . . Zig, Zoey, Connie.'

'Is that all?'

I sat a while longer, hugging the pillow. 'Well, no actually. There's a six.'

'Which is?' he prompted.

'Which is Carter,' I confessed. Reason six was Carter. Now I'd said it out loud and couldn't squash back the way I felt.

'Ah.'

'I know it's down to me that we're not together any more. I mean, we never really were an item . . . you know.'

'Yeah.' Soft, gentle, understanding; that's my dad. Never quick to judge or jump.

'But you realise he's the reason I came back home?'

Dad nodded. By this time he was sitting beside me on the edge of the bed. 'Yeah, I had that figured out.'

'I wanted to talk.'

'And?'

'And I went to his place this evening, but then a girl called Beth arrived . . .'

'Joey has a new girlfriend?' This surprised him. He let it show in his rising voice.

'She's a singer and an actress. She quit West Beck College to turn professional. And she launched a full-scale missile attack on Carter the second she set eyes on him.'

'How do you know all this?'

'Connie gave me the low-down.'

'Hmm, Connie.'

'What does *that* mean? What's wrong with Connie telling me all this stuff about Carter's situation?'

'Nothing,' Dad said, even more thoughtful than before. 'Only, Connie Oseles is hardly an impartial witness, in case you hadn't noticed.'

'How come?' What was Dad trying to say?

'Listen, Kate, anyone with half a brain can see that Connie herself has a small and ongoing fantasy about Joey.'

'*Connie?*' It was my voice hitting the ceiling now.

'Sure. Connie's been on and off in love with Carter for months!'

'No way, Kate; your father must be crazy!' Methinks

Connie did protest too much when I confronted her with Dad's theory. 'Me and Carter? *Puh-lease!*'

I'd gone to the Ahlberg Centre to find her and have the whole thing out.

I mean, if Connie had been secretly harbouring a passion for Joey, how far could I trust her information on him and Beth?

OK, so maybe the best tactic would have been to go talk to Carter, but picture the humiliation if I had to breathe the same air as him and his girl a second time. Once was enough, let me tell you.

Anyways, I knew where to find Connie, because she told me on the phone that she'd subscribed to a week-long acting course run by a guy called Johnny Hudson.

'He's a hunk,' she'd confided. 'A little moody, maybe, but definitely tall, dark, etcetera.'

Which qualified him absolutely to teach drama to stage-struck girls like Connie.

I arrived at the centre when the class was still in progress. It was all method acting: working yourself into a role by studying the real life scenario behind the character's lines. Like, if you were down to play a homeless bum in a movie, you had to go out there and live on the streets, feel the cold in your bones, the hunger in your belly. Well, I think that's what it's about. Anyway, whatever Mister Hunk Hudson was teaching

51

his class sure did have them all convinced.

'Did you see that demo?' Connie had wowed and sighed as she came to join me after the session. As yet, she had no idea why I'd come. 'Johnny was playing an extract: McMurphy from "One Flew Over The Cuckoo's Nest". You know, the psycho guy in a hospital full of crazies? Jeez, he sure had me hooked!'

I'd glanced across at the teacher; tall, yeah, dark, yeah, handsome – if you like mean and moody. Then I'd come straight to the point. 'Connie, do you have a thing for Carter?'

'. . . *What?* No way, Kate . . . puh-lease!' All that denial, but a guilty look in her eyes.

'You do, don't you? Why didn't you tell me?'

Connie dropped her defences and sat me down in a dark corner of the artificially bright studio so that she could come clean. 'OK, even if it's true, what was I supposed to do? Come out with it face to face? "Kate, I know you won't mind if I tell you that I fancy your guy." '

'Carter wasn't my guy.'

She cocked one eyebrow and squinted sideways at me. 'So why are we here?'

'OK, so I wanted Carter to be upfront about his feelings for me. I was still working on it when this thing happened with Matt Kemp.'

'Did Carter know you were working on it?' Connie can be blunt when she's cornered. 'Like, did you ever let him know how you really felt?'

I shook my head and stared at my feet.

Connie broke the short silence with a brilliant piece of self-defence. I'm certain she's gonna make a great attorney one day. 'The way I see it, I acted pretty damn decently. I held off saying a word about Carter to you until you jetted off to New York. Then, when I heard you were partying like crazy with the stars, I thought, "This is my chance!" I made a move on Joey. And guess what: he wasn't interested! Not a flicker.'

I listened hard, imagined the play Connie might have made. I half-smiled when I thought of Carter desperately avoiding Connie's advances.

'Yeah, right!' Connie was a mind-reader as well as a superb logician. 'Very funny.'

'No, I didn't mean . . . I'm sorry.' By now I was convinced that she didn't step out of line until I gave her good reason, i.e. until I'd told her about Matt Kemp's interest in me. After all, Connie and me went way back. We'd never do the dirty.

'No, I'm the one who's sorry,' she sighed. She sat, elbows on her knees, resting her chin in her hands. 'Look at the way Carter's acting now.'

This startled me; I mean, I hadn't expected to run

into Joey here. But there he was, killing the studio lights behind the lighting console. And who was there in the booth with him? You guessed it: Beth Harvey.

They were real cosy. She had an arm round his shoulder and was nibbling his left ear. He was resisting, but not strongly. I saw Johnny Hudson break away from his students and stride across the studio, open the door of the booth and speak to Beth; something about next day's workshops. Carter killed the last of the studio lights and left us in darkness.

'Hey!' some kids shouted. 'Who turned out the lights?'

Carter flicked on the dim house-lights in time for me to make out Beth and Johnny leaving the booth and heading for an office on the opposite side of the studio. Hudson was doing his moody bit, stamping off, and little blonde Beth was tripping along after him.

'Are you sure Carter's into this thing with Beth?' I asked Connie. Like, he hadn't looked altogether comfortable with her ear-nibbling stunt.

Connie gave me a pitying look. 'Yeah, that would be nice,' she agreed. 'If Joey didn't reciprocate the feeling, we'd all be a lot happier. But forget it, Kate. I can tell you straight: the way Beth Harvey sees it, she and Carter are practically engaged!'

* * *

So I sat on a plane back to New York.

I felt empty inside.

I'd done all the beating myself up I could take; blamed myself, called myself names, swore never to date another man as long as I lived.

Dad had taken one look at me when I got back from the Ahlberg Centre and read everything there was to know in my face. 'Sorry, honey,' was all he said.

When I asked for the air fare to JFK, he picked up the phone and reserved the ticket on his debit card. He even called Mom and told her to pick me up from the airport.

'This is a big decision,' he reminded me as he saw me through the check-in desk at Fortune City International. 'Are you sure you're doing the right thing?'

I guess he pictured me running back into Matt Kemp's arms, now that Carter was permanently off the map.

I nodded, kissed his cheek and picked up my bag. The last I saw of Dad was him waving me down the moving walkway, hand raised, looking real uptight.

Then I was on the plane above the clouds. I was floating, hollow, sick in my stomach at what I had to do next.

So I forced myself to focus, to rehearse what I would say to Matt.

I needed to be face to face, to look him in those beautiful blue eyes.

'This isn't working out,' I would tell him, trying to keep my voice calm as I dumped the most eligible actor in America. 'I'm not committed to this relationship. I'm sorry, Matt, but I can't come to Nepal. In fact, I guess it's best if we don't see each other any more.'

5

You'd think in the evening the heat would let up. But no, the streets held the sun's rays like an oven and there was no breeze to lift the stickiness.

When I walked Beth to her audition with Synergie that Monday night, my T-shirt stuck to my shoulders and my hand in hers was slippy with sweat.

Dead romantic; yeah.

'You'll do great,' I told her at least six times. I mean, she was nervous as a kitten, saying she'd never be able to make it through the door, let alone give it her best shot.

'Carter, you'll stay with me, won't you?' She gripped my slimy hand harder. 'I need you to be there.'

Which caught me between a rock and a hard place, since Marcie had already made it clear to me that Beth's audition was band business and I ought to butt out of it.

The venue was the recording studio next to the North Central station on the Circle Train line. My plan was to walk her there, slide off to McDonalds for a burger, come back, walk her home as usual. But she was a hard girl to say no to.

'You'll come in?' she pleaded when we reached the studio door, giving me an appealing kitten look intended to leave me helpless.

It worked, naturally. 'OK, but this is down to you,' I reminded her, shuffling uneasily down the corridor after her. 'If you sing good, you're in. If not . . . I don't feature in this scene, OK!'

If Beth was figuring that because Marcie was my sister then I would have some influence, she really was on a loser. It may have been harsh of me to impute this motive, but with Beth I was beginning to suspect stuff. I mean, she was only helpless when it suited her. Other times, she had a will of iron.

Like when she stood in front of a microphone and sang. Feet apart, deadpan expression, in-your-face. Not a rich, feeling voice; more aggressive, hard-edged. So what happened to the earlier nerves?

Ocean was into this style, obviously. He was there for the audition, along with Marcie and the two other band members, Jimmi G and Andy Casey, who'd just sailed through drug rehab and come out clean. The two guys were hanging out after a day's recording, looking a little pale and jaded, unshaven and like they both needed a drink.

But they sat up when Beth put on the headphones and opened her mouth, watching her from behind the control board while Ocean played with sound levels and got the best out of Beth's voice. Like I say, I'd made myself part of the furniture in the control room, so I was able to observe the band's reaction to Beth's performance without anyone noticing.

Except Marcie, who gave me the dead eye when I walked in because I'd ignored what she'd said.

And she still looked like she wasn't impressed. She listened to what the guys said about Beth – strong voice, good image, sexy – then had her say.

'She's not right for us.' Straight down the line, no fooling around.

'How come?' Ocean was ready for an argument.

Meanwhile Beth came to the end of her song and stood inside the sound booth awaiting their verdict.

'Too hard,' was Marcie's comment. 'The sound doesn't complement our lyrics.'

Synergie had built their name on sensitive, heartfelt stuff, very personal and open. Material by Ocean which came out of his love affair with Marcie. So I took her point.

So did Jimmy G. He made out like he didn't have a strong opinion, but if they pushed him he would agree with Marcie.

Which left only Andy to make a decision. 'She looks good,' he remarked, glancing at my sister to see if this was part of her objection to Beth becoming their backing singer. Like, she could be jealous.

'She looks great,' Marcie admitted. 'All I'm saying is, her voice doesn't sound sincere. With our stuff, you have to mean what you sing.'

Andy grunted, then nodded. His next glance took in me lurking by the door.

'Forget Joey,' Marcie cut in. 'He's not here, are you, Joey?'

I shuffled and shook my head. Invisible man.

All this time, Beth was still waiting, headphones slung around her neck, biting her lip as the band came to a decision.

'The kid will make a great backing singer,' Ocean insisted.

'Yeah, but not with us.' Marcie dug in for a fight. It was good to know that she and Ocean might be in love, but they didn't have to agree over everything.

'Maybe she needs this break. We could get her to soften her style.'

'Ocean, there are a hundred girls out there who look this good, whose voices already do what we want them to do, without re-training.'

'Right . . .' Jimmi mumbled, like he was ready to go home.

So they all looked to Andy for his casting vote.

'I'm with Marcie and Jimmi on this one,' he told Ocean, finally unhooking his jacket from the back of a chair and splitting. 'Sorry, Joey!'

It wasn't me they needed to say sorry to, it was Beth. The poor kid was wiped out by the rejection.

'What did I do?' she asked me all the way to her place after we left the studio. We took the train from the city centre over to East Village, then walked the final couple of blocks.

'You didn't do anything. It's down to Synergie's style.' I tried to convince her that this had nothing to do with the quality of her voice *per se*.

'Carter, I wanted it to work out so bad!'

I put my arm round her shoulder and walked her along. What could I say?

'It was Marcie, wasn't it?' Beth had picked up the correct vibes. 'She was the one who turned me down.'

'I can't tell you anything about that; it puts me in a difficult position, don't you see?'

'It was Marcie,' she concluded. 'If it had been down to Ocean, I'd have got the job.'

And nothing I said would alter Beth's opinion, mainly because it happened to be true.

So we reached her place at an all-time low, with Beth implying that I could've worked harder with Marcie on her behalf, and me suspecting that this had been the set-up all along; ie, that I had only been interesting to Beth as a way of getting an intro to members of Synergie.

Like, she picked up pretty early that I had connections in the music industry because I was dumb enough to tell her so. And she'd been using me ever since.

Well, if it was true, it had backfired. So where did that leave us, relationship-wise?

Off-balance, that's where. I was ready to split at the top of her fire escape. She was crying that she'd lost her big chance, not caring if I came in or not.

Then she saw the rose on the doorstep and went nuts.

I mean, crazy; coming on with the tears, losing it totally. 'Oh God, I can't take any more of this! This guy follows me everywhere. What do I do to get him out of my hair?'

Which guy? I leaned over the fire escape just to check. And sure enough, there was the man in motor-cycle leathers and helmet, making a speedy exit down the iron stairs. We must have crossed paths with him on the way up to Beth's apartment and he'd had to sneak into a dark corner to hide. What you might call a close shave.

'Wait here!' I told Beth. I reckoned I had a chance of catching up with her stalker before he made it to the silver machine parked at the far end of the alleyway.

Not a smart move, you're thinking: chasing after a big, fit guy on a motor-bike. What's more, he was probably crazy. Red roses, hiding in shadows, obsessively stalking the object of his affections.

So, I should've let him ride away.

Instead, I was taking the fire escape steps two at a time, pounding after him. He was glancing back up at me, wondering whether to stay and fight or continue his getaway.

Probably being the jealous, obsessive type made him choose the former.

I jumped the final half dozen steps on to him, flinging myself with all my weight and causing him to stagger off balance. The shell of his helmet crashed against the opposite wall and he slumped under me and hit the ground.

I was still on my feet, holding back this urge to kick him in the ribs. *Mean idea, Carter.*

So instead, I let him struggle up, and the guy came at me like he wanted to bite my head clean off my shoulders. At the last split second, he lowered his head and butted me in the stomach.

I felt the breath leave my body. There was cracking pain in my ribcage and it was my turn to stagger.

'Stop!' Beth came flying down the fire escape, wailing and crying. 'Quit it, you two. Someone's gonna get hurt!'

Too late; I was hurt already, bending double, struggling for breath. My opponent was lashing out with legs and arms, kicking, punching, aiming karate chops at the back of my neck.

I reeled sideways against the metal stairs, slumped against the rail, felt more thuds to my stomach and groin. Man, I was through that pain barrier, doubled up, ready to lose consciousness.

'Johnny, back off!' Beth arrived and threw herself at my assailant. 'Look at what you've done!'

Blood was pouring from my nose, I couldn't breathe, the world was spinning around; sky was earth, apartment blocks lay horizontal.

'Johnny'? Did Beth say a name? Johnny? Or was that my imagination?

The guy in the helmet stopped kicking me at last. He stepped back, wrenched at his visor in order to draw fresh air into his lungs. As he pulled, he raised the whole helmet for me to get the first view of his face.

And yeah, Beth had called him Johnny. I stared hard, with something of a delayed reaction because of lack of oxygen to my brain. Yeah; Johnny Hudson from the Ahlberg Centre was the mystery rose fetishist.

'Get out of here!' Beth yelled at him. 'You hear me, Johnny? You're way out of line this time!'

He sucked in air, staring at me like he did truly want to end my life. He enjoyed the blood, the bruises, the victory.

But then Beth's voice got through to him.

'I'll call the cops!' she warned. (Maybe an idea that should have entered her head a whole lot sooner.)

Hudson quit sneering at me and backed off a couple of feet.

'I mean it, Johnny. I'll have you thrown in jail if you don't quit this whole crazy game!'

He might be an obsessed weirdo, but he still didn't want to end up behind bars. So he nodded and grunted, shoving his helmet back on and retreating down the alleyway.

'Get up, Carter!' Beth hissed at me. By this time, a couple of neighbours had emerged on to the fire escape landings. They weren't sufficiently interested to interfere, only to observe. A non-paying audience.

'I'm trying!' Pushing myself upright, I swayed forward, staggered two paces, swayed back, wishing the world would stay put around me. At last I managed to drag air into my lungs, at the same time yelping at the pain in my ribs.

'Lean on me. I'll get you up the steps.' Beth guided me on the agonising journey up ten flights of stairs. You have to remember, every joint in my body ached; not like in the old movies when the cowboy gets beaten to a pulp, then leaps right on his horse and gallops after the bandits. No way. The real thing is different.

65

'It's OK, Carter, you can make it.' Beth eased me along, past the nosy neighbours.

'You want I should call a doctor?' one woman asked anxiously. She was an overweight redhead of maybe forty-five, cigarette in her hand, wearing faded pink lip-gloss.

'No, he's OK . . . thanks.' Beth supported me on up the next flight.

I was? So what was the red sticky stuff on my T-shirt? Why did my jaw feel like it was broken in three places? 'Uh-uh-uh!' I mumbled.

'Don't talk, Carter. Come inside. I'll get you cleaned up.' Beth bundled me out of sight through the door to her apartment.

'So?' I asked.

My bloodied T-shirt was in the trash-can; I was sitting stripped to the waist on Beth's sofa, watching the red marks on my body turn to blue bruises. No bones broken, so far as I could tell. But throbbing and aching all over my body; yeah, plenty of that.

'So what?' She stood with her back to the window, framed against the darkening sky.

'So Johnny Hudson is your stalker. You knew that all along.'

Can a stalker be a stalker if you know who he is? Yeah, I guess so. Only, why hadn't Beth identified him to the cops and got the guy off her back?

She shrugged and turned to look out of the window.

'You lied to me about him.'

'Yeah, sorry, Carter.'

'How come you gave me this story about the mystery rose-man and it turns out to be someone you knew all along?' Speech was difficult through swollen and cut lips, but I was doing my best.

Beth turned back into the room. She stuck by the window, confronting the issue of lying to me across a table scattered with books on theatre and acting. The walls of the room were painted bright yellow; there were giant paper sunflowers in a zinc bucket, posters of recent Fortune City Theatre productions on the walls. 'I reckoned Johnny's obsession with me was harmless,' she explained. 'In a way, it was kinda flattering.'

Like, yeah! Flattering enough for me to sustain a broken jaw over. OK, so I'm exaggerating.

'Listen, Johnny and me, we go way back,' Beth went on. 'It's complicated, but the bottom line is that we dated while I was at college. He taught part-time at West Beck, remember. Our relationship had to be kept secret because of college rules, but it was good at first. Then later it grew to be bad news. He was jealous of me talking to boys my own age, wouldn't leave me alone, kept on calling late at night – that kind of stuff.'

'So you broke it off?' I guessed.

'Yeah, but it sent Johnny off the rails. I mean, he's an intense kind of a guy. First, he threatened to commit suicide. Then he messed up his job at the college by not showing up for lectures. There was no salary coming in, only the money he earned as a session musician, playing guitar in small clubs like the Lemon House. I mean, it's the story of Johnny's life actually – lots of talent both as an actor and a musician, but throwing it all away over some crazy fixation.'

'He's done this kind of thing before?' Was this guy seriously weird, or not?

Beth nodded. 'So, he has no steady money and he gets thrown out of his apartment. By this time, I've quit college myself, but I hear he's on the street. And it's about this time that the red roses start arriving.'

'Did you guess Hudson was behind them from the start?' Hudson with the heavy fists and big boots, with that manic look in his eyes.

'Maybe. I didn't really care. I stuck the flowers in a vase on the kitchen shelf and never thought about it.'

'And what's the guy on? Is it alcohol? Drugs?'

'In his time he's gone through everything you ever heard of, and more. He hits rock-bottom, but then he straightens himself out. He gets back into playing the clubs, doing a little teaching . . .'

'But he still has this thing for you?' I put in. Now it made sense how Hudson was mean and moody at the Ahlberg Centre. He would see Beth making the play for me and it would drive him wild. More roses, more resentment. No wonder he almost kicked me to death down there.

'Forget it, Carter, why don't you? Life's too short.'

Which was playing things pretty cool, if you asked me. Here was I hurting all over and she was telling me she didn't plan to do anything about Hudson's violent assault. 'I thought he creeped you out. Or did I get that part wrong too?'

Remember the spooky underpass, the please-walk-me-home scenario.

This whole thing was starting to seriously upset me. 'As a matter of fact, while we're not pulling any punches, is there anything else I may have misunderstood?'

'Like what, Carter?' Beth stood with her arms folded across her chest. I would have to describe the expression on her face as pouting, sulking, moody, mean, defensive-aggressive; you take your pick of adjectives that mean her bottom lip is pushed slightly forward of the top lip and there are frown lines between her eyes.

'Like the reason you got it together with me in the first place. It couldn't have anything to do with you furthering your own career, could it?'

69

She laughed out loud. I guess she thought this was an oddball way to describe it. 'You got that right,' she confessed. 'What other reason would I have for dating someone like you?'

Now I was mad. I mean, who the hell did Beth Harvey think she was? I got up from the sofa, planning to walk right out of that crummy apartment.

My legs let me down though. They practically seized up on me and refused to cover the ground.

'It's not as though you're God's gift to women, Joey, now is it?'

Jeez, had I been a sucker. Beth had fluttered her eyelids and I'd fallen for the whole stupid game.

And messed up with Kate when she came back to Fortune City to talk. That's what drove me *really* crazy.

'I'm outta here,' I muttered through my puffed-up lips. I made my feet move one in front of the other. More of a stumble than a walk.

'Fine!' Beth watched me struggle. 'Oh, and Carter, the way I see it, I'm the one who broke off this crummy relationship, OK!'

'OK, no problem, tell it whatever way you like.' *Only let me out of here!* The rug swam up towards my eyes, the zig-zag pattern played havoc with my balance. I guess I swayed and stumbled some more.

The last I remember, I was out on the tenth-floor

landing of the fire escape, and now it was the ground hundreds of feet below that was racing up to meet me and the moonlit sky was criss-crossed with more shooting stars than you ever saw. Or maybe that was just me. Whatever. I noticed Mrs-You-Want-I-Should-Call-A-Doctor emerge on to a landing below then saw her red hair and pink lip-gloss kind of float up towards me, asking in an echoing voice, was I OK?

'Sure,' I mumbled. 'I'm doing real good, thanks.'

Then I must have passed out.

At least, that's what they told me later.

6

This may be a girl-thing, but I was real scared of hurting Matt's feelings.

I mean, how do you finish a relationship without coming across as a bitch?

I rehearsed all the ways during the plane trip back to New York: 'Matt, I'm sorry, but finishing school is a priority for me.' (True, but too geeky.) 'Matt, I can't keep up with your life-style. I'm not into clothes and good haircuts and driving red convertibles along the coast road.' (Not true; I'm as addicted to designer labels as the next girl.) 'Matt, this isn't gonna work out. I'll throw up my entire future, and come tomorrow you'll meet some super-glamorous actress or fashion model, and as far as you're concerned I'll be history.' (Closer. I could see myself stranded up a mountain in Nepal with only my memories and no plane ticket home.)

Or finally, a sentence that cut through all the other garbage and told it like it really was. 'Matt, I'm in love with someone else.'

There, I'd said it. I was in love with someone else.

Not just anyone, but Carter. Joey Carter. I'd known it for a while now, but going out with Matt had finally sorted everything out in my head. Only now I wasn't ever going to be able to tell him. Joey, that is. Matt was a different story altogether. Would his fragile ego be crushed? Fragile? You must be kidding. This guy is a movie actor, remember. They have egos thick as rhinoceros hide. And the in-love-with-someone-else thing was where it was at. I mean, really. Now that Carter had got himself another girl, I could acknowledge how deep my feeling for him went. Like they say, you don't know what you've got until it's gone.

'Matt, I'm in . . . I mean, er, listen to me just a second . . . I want to tell you something.'

During the real event, it proved hard to get a word in edgeways.

Matt flew back from LA and met up with me at Mom's gallery, shortly after she'd picked me up from JFK.

'I'll leave you two kids alone,' she told us sweetly, imagining a tender reunion. And she went off for sushi with Val Cominesci.

'This is the biggest deal!' Matt was enthusing about his new movie contract. 'They want to pull in a whole string of "A" list actors, but I still get top billing. My name above the title, a cut of any profit the movie makes worldwide . . .'

He'd had a haircut in LA and put blond streaks into the dark crop. He looked surfer-cool, very toned and tanned. I tried not to picture him sitting for an hour in the hairstylist's chair wearing a pierced plastic cap, smelling of chemical dye.

Five minutes into the conversation, he noticed it was me he was talking to. 'Hey, Kate, what happened to the cream Donna Karan number? How come the casual, off-duty look?

I glanced down at my pale blue vest-top and creased linen trousers rolled halfway up to my knees for coolness. My feet peeped out of comfortable beige leather sandals. It was how I'd stepped off the plane from Fortune City. 'This is the way I usually look,' I told him. And suddenly I didn't feel like apologising for that.

Matt frowned like he'd remembered something he needed to tell me. Less important than the movie deal, obviously. But still an issue he needed to deal with.

'Hey, Kate; you know that plan about you flying out to Nepal to visit me on set?'

I nodded. I pictured an executioner's block, heard the smooth slide of the guillotine as it descended towards my neck.

'Yeah well, forget about that, huh? I mean, nice idea at the time, but since Honor-Lee broke up with Kris, she and I got kinda close . . . y'know.'

'You did?' I yelped. It was anger, not hurt. With myself. I mean, how come I let Matt do the dumping? Because I was pussyfooting around trying to deal with his imaginary hurt feelings, that's why. Like I say, guys don't seem to have the same problem. *Whoosh*, straight in with the knife!

'Yeah, Honor-Lee was out in LA doing her own movie deal. She hit on me pretty hard, if you must know.'

'Did you and she appear in the newspaper yet?'

Ping! My poisoned arrow hit the rhinoceros hide and bounced right off.

'OK, so I have to go meet a couple of guys for lunch.' Matt took one more dismissive look at my non-label shoes. He was already walking off between the paintings and abstract, post-modernist metal sculptures. 'They're the money men, the studio moguls. Gotta go, OK?' *Exit, stage left.*

I was sitting alone in the white space.

I was wanting to laugh.

Then suddenly I cried.

That was how Mom found me when she came back from the Japanese place around the corner.

'Kate honey, what happened?' Putting her arm round me, she hustled me away from public view. Not that anyone had come into the gallery while she was away. And anyhow, maybe I was a live exhibit: 'Girl Crying'. Concept art.

'Did Matt upset you?' Mom asked in her small office. She pushed black coffee into my hands, looped my hair behind my ears and stroked my cheek. 'Listen, it happens. Guys can be pretty thoughtless sometimes. You have to get through it and not let them see you're hurt.'

She obviously thought the rift was temporary, so I told her straight. 'Matt broke it off.'

'Oh Kate, no!'

'Oh Mom, yes!' Major tragedy. Forget the wedding outfit, the ten-page spread in *Hello* magazine.

She went silent; a rare event. When she spoke, her voice had changed to low and sympathetic. 'Honey, I'm sorry. C'mon, don't cry. He isn't worth it.'

I looked up through my tears. 'Say that again.'

'I said, Matt Kemp isn't worth crying over. OK, so he looks like he's got it made. But y'know, he comes across a pretty superficial type of guy. And egocentric. You'd spend your life feeding his ego, I guess.'

'You don't mind?' I stammered.

'Sure, I mind. I care that he has a head so full of his

beautiful, talented self that he can't see the genuine article. I mean, honey, any guy in this world would take one look at you and fall at your feet. And I'm not only talking physical appearance here; I'm pointing out the fact that you're one great kid – genuine, honest, kind, smart . . .'

'Mom, stop!' I was crying even harder.

'Honey!' She started with the tears too, giving me the biggest hug I ever had from her.

I tell you, people constantly surprise me.

'Anyhow, I'm not crying over stupid Matt Kemp,' I confessed. Truth time. Mother and daughter stuff.

'No?' She pulled a box of tissues out of a drawer, handed one to me, used one herself to dab around her mascara.

'No. I'm crying about Carter.'

'Joey? Where does he fit in?' Mom blew her nose, sat upright, smoothed her skirt.

'He fits in here.' I put both hands across my heart. 'I love him, Mom. And guess what? He went and got himself a new girl.'

'So, call him and tell him how you feel!' Mom said, as soon as she'd digested the facts.

I felt my heart leap into my mouth. You know that sensation? A great surge in your chest, followed by the inability to swallow. I shook my head and felt faint.

'Sure, call him.' She dived into my purse for my cell phone, looked up Joey's number, punched the buttons.

I carried on protesting with grunts and moans.

'Trust me,' she said, handing me the phone as it started to ring.

Don't be there! I pleaded silently. *Be out playing basketball with Zig! Be anywhere so I don't have to go through with this conversation!*

But Mom kept an eagle eye on me as the dial tone kept on. 'Be brave!' she mouthed. 'Tell him how you feel!'

Someone picked up the phone in Twenty-second Street. 'Marcie Carter speaking.'

'Hey, Marcie. Kate here.' I was off the hook; I could safely back out of the most difficult phone call of my entire life.

Like: *Hey, Carter. How're you doing? Listen, Mom says I have to call and tell you I love you. Yeah, I know; I left it too late. You found someone else. She's everything you ever wanted in a girl. Yeah, sorry to bother you. Bye.*

'Kate, where are you? I've been trying to call you at your place all morning.'

Marcie sounded worried, like something big had happened. So much so that I forgot about the hard time I was having trying to dream up exactly what I would say to Carter. 'Why, what happened?'

'It's Joey. He got into a fight.'

'Is he hurt? How bad?' Now my heart had sunk and was jumping around behind my ribs. *How bad? How bad? How bad?*

'He's OK. They just beat him up pretty rough.'

'Who's "they"?' *Carter, why can't you stay out of trouble? Why do you do this to me?*

'Well, "he" actually.' Marcie came in with a rapid string of facts to put me out of my misery. 'It's a guy who's been stalking Beth Harvey. She told Carter about him and her story was that she needed protection from a mystery fanatic who leaves her red roses all the time. You know Joey, he's a sucker that way.'

'He got into a fight over Beth?' *Let me get this straight. This wasn't sounding good from my point of view.*

'Yeah. Only, it turns out that the stalker isn't a mystery man after all. It's some weirdo Beth knows. She used to date him. In fact, I happen to know the guy too.'

'Who is he?' *Trust Carter. Yeah, good old gullible Joey. See a damsel in distress, and he's up there on his white charger.*

Marcie filled me in on all the details. 'His name's Johnny Hudson. He's a musician and drama teacher with a serious drink problem compounded with a personality disorder that makes him fixate on girls younger than himself. That's only my opinion, you understand. Not a medical diagnosis. Only, I've seen this guy from close-up.'

'How come?'

'Hudson got involved with the band way back. He used to hang out with Jimmi G, then when Synergie began to get it together, Johnny tried to jump on our bandwagon. He came to us with the lyrics to a song he wanted us to record, but Ocean turned him down flat. It happens to us a lot: guys wanting a slice of our action.'

'So then Hudson held some sort of grudge?' I prompted, still not seeing the connection with Joey being beaten to a pulp.

'Yeah, he acted slightly weird. I think he even threatened Jimmi with a knife when he was drunk. Jimmi shrugged it off, didn't take it any further. Then the guy decides he's going to sue us because we bring out a track six months later which he says is his song and he has copyright.'

'Did he get any money?'

'No way. Our lawyers got it thrown out before it got to court. So, yeah, there's an unhinged guy with a violent streak somewhere out there bearing a grudge. He's also, as it happens, fixated on the girl my kid brother's hanging out with.'

This is where my heart lurched again, but I kept quiet and told it to go on beating normally.

'Now, I don't know if Hudson made the connection, and that's what made him kick the heck out of Joey last night . . .'

'Ouch!'

'It's OK, Kate. I'm only telling you this to keep you up to speed before I hand you over to my brother who's hanging over the phone even as we talk. He spent the night in hospital, but he walked out on his own two feet. You might find his voice a little strange, on account of a busted lip, that's all.'

'Thanks, Marcie. Can I talk to Carter now?'

'Here he is . . .'

There was a crackly pause as the receiver changed hands. I heard Joey tell Marcie to butt out, he wanted a private talk with me.

I put my hand over the mouthpiece and asked Mom to do the same, only more politely.

'Tell it like it is,' was her maternal advice as she left the office.

'Hey, Carter,' I began. *Breathless. Butterflies in the stomach. No way could I go through with this.*

'Hey.'

'How're you doing?'

'Take no notice of Marcie. She's hyping the whole thing up.'

'You don't sound too good.'

'I got a lip the size of a tennis-ball is all.'

'That's OK then.' I tried to make light of things. 'Listen, I'm glad Marcie filled me in. Knowing you, you would've told me you fell over in a ball game.'

'So why did you call?' he asked.

Tough question. The one I was dreading. 'I wanted to say sorry, Carter.' There! Not so painful now that it was done. Somehow I could do this long distance easier than face to face. Even if Joey told me that he accepted my apology but it was too late – he had Beth to consider now – I thought I could handle it.

There was a long silence. 'Sorry for what?' he mumbled.

'For the whole Matt Kemp thing. I never should've got involved.'

Silence.

'It's over, Carter.' Spell it out; set the record straight.

'You ended it with him?'

'No, I planned to but I didn't get the chance. It was a case of "the ego has landed"!'

'*He* ended it with *you?*'

'It was a mutual thing. I decided to stay in school. He found someone else. We called it quits.'

'You're gonna come back to Fortune City?' Checking, double-checking. Cautious Carter.

'For the fall semester.' *OK, Kate; do it. Tell him how you really feel* . . . Silence.

'Yeah,' he said with a sigh that sounded like relief. 'I got news for you too.'

'Yeah?' We were both whispering, both hesitating, finding our way through.

'I threw in the towel with Beth.'

'Meaning?'

'Meaning, she showed up at the hospital late this morning. A woman downstairs from Beth's apartment was the one who scraped me up off the floor and called the ambulance. Beth didn't show at my bedside for twelve whole hours. I mean, where was she? Anyhow, I already decided to break things off. Her visiting my sickbed just gave me the chance to do it nice and clean.'

'You broke off with Beth?' My turn to echo him. Double, triple-checking.

'Yeah, and I'm sorry I was such a sucker over her,' Carter told me.

The sorries were whizzing around now. I was sorry. He was sorry. Neither of us had a new partner any more.

Tell him, Kate. Don't lose it now.

'Joey, I'm sorry you got beaten up.' My voice was

83

real low and slow. 'And there's something else . . .'

'Yeah, I know.'

'You know?'

'Yeah. You don't need to spell it out.'

'Spell what out?' He refused to use the four-letter word. L-O-V-E.

We ended without either of us admitting it. But we both knew in our hearts.

And, wow, was I flying, floating free, dreaming, loving life when Mom walked back into her office.

What Carter had actually said was he'd more or less lost the will to live while Hudson was kicking him around the alleyway.

'It didn't matter. Nothing mattered. Without you, I couldn't care less what happened to me,' he'd confessed. He'd also said that he didn't regret the few days he'd spent with Beth Harvey, since it had only gone to prove to him what the real thing had been like with me.

'Same at this end,' I'd told him, as regards Matt Kemp.

So we'd ended on a high – me telling Carter not to get himself beaten up any more, him promising to take more care just so long as I got myself back where I belonged.

'Which is?' I'd asked. Sometimes you have to push a

guy like Carter to the point where he actually comes out with what you want to hear.

'Which is here with me,' he told me. *Upfront. No fooling around. Carter and me.*

And so Mom put me back on a plane to Fortune City first thing Wednesday morning. My plan was to take a cab from the airport, straight over to Twenty-second Street and surprise the life out of my poor, beaten-up, busted-lip boyfriend.

7

Beth Harvey taught me a lot. Like, dating girls you didn't previously know was riskier than any extreme sport you care to name. Here was me with a busted lip and bruises all over my body, confined to the house on a day hot enough to grill burgers on the sidewalk.

Forget snowboarding, bungee-jumping or white-water rafting. Make a wrong move as far as girls are concerned, and you could end up dead.

Not that I was in regretful mode. Oh no. I was going round the place smiling as much as my lip would allow. I was singing snatches from Synergie's last CD – 'Mystery to me . . . mystery to me . . .' – making jokes with Damien and tickling Fern until she went crazy.

'Joey, take it easy,' Mom warned as she left for work. 'I want you here in the house so I can call to make regular checks that you're OK.'

I shrugged and hummed some more.

'What got into him?' Mom asked Marcie.

My sister gave a knowing grin. 'Lurve!' she growled. 'That's what happened to him!'

'Lurve, lurve, lurve . . . Lurve is all you need!' Humming, sashaying round the kitchen on my aching joints, making Fern laugh.

Then I went up to my room to check my e-mails again. Kate would be sending messages on the net, telling me about her plans for the day, how she felt that her and me were meant to be.

Or she would be calling. I would pick up the phone and hear her voice.

But hey, nothing!

I mean, no telephone call, no e-mail. Zilch all through Wednesday morning.

To say I was let down is an understatement. By midday I felt like committing a self-destructive act, I can tell you.

Maybe I was accessing the wrong address. Sit down at the p.c., try again. Log on, type in Kbrennan@aol.com Decide to send a message. Change my mind, stand up, sit down, check my new messages.

There was one, but not from Kate.

You should've stayed away from Beth, jerk.
Too late now. You're in real deep.
Way out of your depth, kid.
How did it feel when the boot went in? How much did it hurt?
Not half so much as it's gonna hurt next time.
Watch your back, sonny. And be afraid.

Unsigned, except for a piece of clip-art showing a single rose. Hudson's unique signature.

Twenty-four hours earlier, I wouldn't have cared. I would've dragged my battered body out to the nearest dark corner and waited for the stalker to pounce. I mean, my spirits had sunk that low.

But today was different. Today I wanted to live real bad.

'Problem, Joey?' Marcie stuck her head around my door and saw me shake from head to foot.

I deleted the stalker's message. *Zap*. My screen saver was a clip-art axe covered in blood. My idea of a joke. Funny, huh? 'No problem,' I lied.

'Yeah, like nothing's brought you out in a cold sweat!' My big sister had nothing better to do than bug me, obviously. 'C'mon, Joey, what was that you had on-screen?'

'Nothing.'

'Joey!'

'I'm OK. Butt out, will ya.'

'Bring up that message again.' Marcie grabbed me by the bruised left shoulder.

'Hey, that hurt!'

'Message, Joey!'

Ouch, ouch. 'OK, OK!' I pressed a few keys and brought up Hudson's loving missive. '. . . *In real deep . . . not half so much as it's gonna hurt next time . . . Be afraid!'*

Marcie gasped as she read it. 'Jeez, Joey!'

She ran straight for the phone to call the cops. Emergency. My kid brother just received a death threat. What-are-you-gonna-do-about it?

'Cool it, lady,' the cop said. 'A million nuts a day send crazy messages on the internet. If we responded to everything we got told about, we'd need to triple the size of our police department.'

Or words to this effect.

'Listen, sergeant: Joey just got beaten to a pulp last night. We already reported that. This is no ordinary crazy guy; this is someone who acts out his fantasy for real!' Marcie refused to lie down and die in front of the cop's chugging train of cynicism.

'Yeah, and you listen, lady. I'm adding it to the file here on my computer. "Received: one piece of electronic hate-mail from unknown sender."'

'Correction!' she stepped in smartly. 'Identity of hate-mail sender is known to victim. We know it's the same guy as last night because he was kind enough to leave his trademark signature. A rose.'

Still this didn't impress the desk sergeant. 'OK, so let me get my head around this. The crazy guy follows up an assault by making a death threat against your kid brother. And, for good measure, he identifies who he is?'

'That's what I said.'

'Smart move on his part, wouldn't you say?'

'Yeah, I know it's illogical. But I'm telling you, sergeant: Johnny Hudson is seriously crazy.'

'And I'm writing down his name on my file here a second time – H-U-D-S-O-N. And I guess you want us to go out there and make an arrest?'

'Well, I did figure that beating a kid to within an inch of his life was a federal offence,' Marcie said, real sarcastic. 'I'd say it warrants police action, wouldn't you?'

This time the cop had no smart answer.

'So?' she pushed.

'So, I'll put an extra guy on to it soon as I can,' the sergeant conceded at last. 'But so far we don't even have an address for Hudson, and we're already kinda busy, so don't hold your breath.'

Like, it gives you so much faith in the Fortune City Police Department.

Even Marcie couldn't hurry the official response. She would've had armed police on the rooftops opposite the house, a whole raft of detectives out there to track down Johnny Hudson's whereabouts.

She did what she could with the information we had available, then came off the phone.

'That sucks!' was all she said.

90

Then it was time for her to take Fern and Damien to a Disney movie. She'd promised and put them off for three whole days. No way could she call a rain-check again.

'That's fine by me,' I told her. 'You go ahead, get these kids out of my hair.'

'And you don't set foot out of the house!' She hesitated, even while Damien and Fern stampeded for the door.

I gave Marcie a look.

'OK, OK; but I'm seriously concerned for your safety, Joey.'

'And I'm seriously considering throwing this computer monitor at you if you don't get out of here fast!'

This is how we express sibling affection in the Carter family.

Marcie raised her eyebrows, hustled the kids down the steps and slammed the door.

Which left me alone in the house, re-reading my hate-mail and trying to predict what Hudson would do next.

I mean, his type has a definite fanatical streak, so I knew not to judge him by everyday standards. He was the sort to fixate and fuel his obsession with alcohol. If his latest idea was that I was a piece of vermin to be exterminated from the face of the earth because I'd dared to date his darling Beth, then it might not be too long before I, Joey Carter, was history.

And just when things were working out for me, too. *Calling Kate, calling Kate. Come in, please!*

My willpower gave out and I'd just picked up the phone to dial New York when there was a hammering on the front door.

Oh shoot; that must be the movie-goers returning to pick up Damien's eyeglasses which he needed to wear for long-distance. The kid hated them and never told his buddies that he used them.

So I slobbed to answer the urgent knock, ready with the wisecracks, like 'Damien, you'd forget your head if it was loose' – whatever.

I opened the door and Beth Harvey stumbled in.

She was heaving great gulps of air into her lungs, looking over her shoulder, then staggering against me and starting to sob.

'It's OK!' I told her, cranking my stiff arms up to shoulder level to pat her on the back. Then I tried to ease her upright so she wasn't leaning on me.

'Oh God, oh God!' she cried.

The tears smudged her mascara and the wet stain trickled down to the corners of her mouth. I patted her some more until she could finally speak sense.

'He's out there!' she whimpered. 'Oh, Carter, it was horrible! He almost ran me down in the street!'

'Hudson? He drove at you on his Harley?'

She nodded and sagged against me once more. 'I thought I was dead!'

'He tried to kill you?' Man, the guy must have totally lost it this time. 'How did you get away?'

'It was on Franklin Avenue. He rode right across the central reservation and came at me out of nowhere. I had to dive down the subway to get out of his path.'

'Did anyone see it? Have you reported him?' I was trying to think straight. What we needed to do was to get this homicidal maniac behind bars, like fast.

Beth shook her head and sobbed some more. 'It's so hot out there, the streets are dead. Everyone's taking a siesta, I guess.'

'So does Hudson know you headed for my place?'

Another shake of the head. 'No. I don't know. I ran under the dual carriageway and jumped on the Circle Train. Johnny didn't see me, but maybe he would figure it out for himself.'

'You know I got a death threat?' I said, though of course she couldn't possibly.

'You did?' She stood bolt upright with shock, took a deep breath, stopped crying. 'Oh, Carter!'

'Didn't you tell Hudson that you and I were through?' I quizzed. 'I mean, he's e-mailing me crazy messages as if you and me were still an item.'

This set off the tears again. 'When?' she sobbed. 'How

could I let Johnny know? Since he beat you up in the alleyway, no one's seen him.'

'Yeah, course.' This put a deep frown on my face. I was in danger for something I wasn't even doing any more.

Worse still, every item of traffic that passed by down the street outside made me jump clean out of my bruised skin, imagining that it was Hudson on his sleek silver machine. Think about it: an obsessive like him would quickly work out that Beth would come running straight to my house. Single track mind. As far as he was concerned, there were only two people in the whole world: Beth and me.

'You gotta help me, Carter! Johnny's driving me crazy. I don't know what to do!'

Fact: neither did I. 'Let's try calling the cops,' I suggested without conviction. I pictured getting the same desk sergeant down the precinct, who would scarcely be able to stifle a yawn.

Anyhow, that would've taken more time than it turned out we had.

There was a roar of a motorcycle engine out in the street, the skid of tyres. Our stalker had made a none too silent arrival on the scene.

Beth recovered from the shock first. She darted from the hallway down into the basement, looking for a back exit from the building.

I checked through the hall window to see Hudson's Harley abandoned by the sidewalk, then followed my ex-girlfriend. I overtook her to slide open the bolts to the basement door, then let her run out ahead of me into the yard behind the block.

'Take a right!' I yelled. 'Left leads to a dead-end!'

We were both sprinting hard across the yard, thirty yards towards an alley half-blocked by garbage bins and pieces of scrap metal – wrecked bicycle frames, sections of rusting bodywork from autos.

Well, Beth was doing the sprinting. I was creaking and groaning along as best I could. By now, Hudson must be battering down my front door.

And the garbage-strewn alley slowed us both down. We had to climb over the scrap metal and emerge into the hottest, stillest, quietest street you can imagine. Deserted. A bright glare after the shadows, heat rising from the tarmac in shimmering waves.

Then another roar from a motorcycle engine, a metal monster bearing right down on us.

I had time to think, *How come Hudson isn't hammering on my door like we pictured?*

The Harley reflected the sun in a hundred dazzling surfaces; it ate up the road at terrific speed, the volume of the engine grew deafening. Seated on the bike, the leather figure crouched low, his whole concentration on mowing us down.

'In here!' Beth gasped.

She chose a second alleyway to dart down before I'd even got my head together about the fact that Johnny Hudson was several steps ahead of us all the time.

'No: bad idea!' I protested. It was another dead-end.

She didn't listen. I saw the pale flash of her blonde head in the dark shade between the tall buildings, heard the revving engine almost on top of me, then decided to follow her.

Hudson missed me by about a yard. He rode on down the street, the engine fading. Then there were our footsteps in the alley, deep shadows, a man in a chef's uniform opening the back door to a restaurant and throwing out the trash.

I felt like a rat running down the wrong drain, or some other hunted creature cornered down a culvert with the dogs baying behind.

'Turn around. We gotta get out of here!' I yelled at Beth, who had finally paused to wait for me.

She looked strangely calm; not breathless any more, not out of her head with fear.

'What?' I stopped dead, felt my skin begin to crawl.

Beth tilted back her head and gave me a cold smile, eyes half-closed, jaw slightly open.

'Jeez!' Talk about a trapped rat and the wrong drain. I flashed a look behind me in time to see Hudson's leather-clad figure burst through the back door of the restaurant which the chef had just left ajar. 'You set me up!' I gasped.

'Clever, Carter!' Beth enjoyed the outcome every bit as much as a member of the audience at a Broadway show. Each step Johnny Hudson took towards me with the knife in his hand gave her a definite buzz. 'What you gonna do now, Joey?' Like, 'What-(*step*)-you-(*step*)-gonna-(*step*)-do-(*step*)-now?'

The knife? Oh yeah, the knife. It was the long, curved kitchen kind. The type you use to carve meat.

And Hudson was pointing it directly at my throat.

8

I like surprises myself. So I figured Carter would be pleased when I stepped off the plane from New York and showed up on his doorstep unannounced.

'Hey,' I would say when he opened the door.

I would wait for him to handle the shock, run a hand through his mussed-up hair, take a look behind him to see if Fern or Damien were sneaking up. Then he would lean forward to kiss me.

Yeah, that was the big moment I'd had in my mind since we last spoke. The kiss.

It had taken us several lifetimes and a few thousand air-miles, but we were getting there.

Wednesday, 3.30 p.m. I stepped out of the cab to find Twenty-second Street pretty much deserted. Maybe a stray dog or two, a kid sitting on a shady stoop playing with his computer game. Oh, and sun, dust, a shimmering heatwave down the end of the block.

Carter's front door was unlocked, which is unusual in this neighbourhood.

I could be any type of criminal pushing the door

with my fingertips, stepping inside and calling 'Hey!'

'Anybody home?' I tried the kitchen, the living-room, then the basement.

So far, no reply. You know that story of the *Mary Celeste*, the ship they found becalmed on the ocean with not a soul on board? There was food on the tables, drink in the glasses, a map spread out on the captain's deck to chart their course. But there wasn't a sailor to be seen.

Well, 224 Twenty-second Street was like that now. Empty and dreamlike (partly because of the drowsy heat), with everything just dropped where someone had last used it. I found cold coffee in a cup in the kitchen, a newspaper spread out on the low table in the living-room, Damien's glasses sitting on the TV which was playing the cartoon channel with the volume turned down.

Then I went downstairs to check the musical equipment which Marcie and the guys from the band stored down there. That stuff was worth thousands, I knew. It all seemed undisturbed, not a guitar string unstrung or a cable unplugged.

Weird. My feeling by this time was distinctly uneasy. Especially when I saw the basement door out on to the yard also open.

'Hey!' I called again. Maybe someone was out there

catching some cool air. But then again, it wasn't exactly scenic in the Carters' back-yard.

So I closed and bolted the door and went back upstairs. OK, so my next and by this time panicky thought was that Carter might be taking a siesta. Unlikely, but worth a try. I climbed the stairs two at a time, knocked on the door to his room, then quickly pushed it open.

Not so much *Mary Celeste* as post-World War Three. There were clothes, books, bags, sport shoes, baseball bat, empty cups and cans strewn everywhere – typical Carter. Nothing unusual here, then. But I did stop to take a look at the e-mail message on-screen in the only clear corner of the room.

'You should've stayed away from Beth, jerk.

Too late now. You're in real deep.'

Oh Jeez! Pray that this was a joke. Let it not be real. I read through the message to the part where it warned Carter to watch his back and be afraid.

Then, downstairs the front door flew open and Damien and Fern rioted into the house.

Thank God! Here came the explanation. In a few seconds, I would have a grip on the crazy situation.

I flew out of Carter's room to see Marcie following the kids into the hallway. She looked exhausted by the heat, kicking off her shoes and dumping her purse on a ledge at the bottom of the stairs.

'Hey, Kate,' she said, lightening up when she saw me. 'I thought you were in New York.'

'I was. I came to see Joey, but my surprise fell flat on its face.'

'How come?' Marcie sighed and wiggled her bare toes on the cool tiles.

'He's not here,' I told her.

And man, you never saw anyone lose it the way Marcie did then. She performed an action replay of what I'd done, only three times as fast, checking the kitchen, living-room and basement. 'Jeez, I told him not to leave the house! Did you search his room? What took hold of him? How could he be so stupid?'

Marcie going overboard made me calmer. 'Maybe he went to Zig's house?' I suggested, picking up the phone to call and check.

'He'd leave a note. Even Joey would know not to disappear today of all days without saying where he was going.' Marcie ran round the house once, twice, three times.

'What's the problem?' Damien wanted to know, dodging out of his big sister's path, watching my face as I got the information from Zig that no, they hadn't seen Carter but they were planning to call and visit to see how he was.

'Joey vanished,' I told Damien, trying to put on a casual act. 'But hey, he'll show up; no problem.'

So Damien and Fern went to watch cartoons while Marcie faced the fact that she would have to call her parents and drag them out of work. Then the cops. Or the other way around: cops first, Mom and Dad after.

While she hesitated, the phone rang. I darted to answer it.

'Take a message. Listen real good,' a guy said. No introductions, no social manner. This was shooting from the hip. 'I've got Joey Carter. If you want him back without serious damage, you need to hand over five hundred thousand dollars.'

I gripped the phone to stop my hand from shaking. 'Let me talk to Carter!'

The guy laughed. 'Yeah, right!'

'If you don't let him talk, how do I know you're genuine?' I was thinking fast, praying that my judgement was good. My idea was to get to speak with Joey and try to pick up even the smallest clue about what had happened, where he was, who was holding him. A long shot, but possible.

Later, the shock would set in, but right now, my head was clear.

'OK, you win,' the voice told me. 'Let me ease this

gag a little. Here you go, Carter. Tell the little lady about your predicament.'

I heard some fumbling, then Joey's muffled, cautious words. 'Who's that?'

'Carter, it's me, Kate.'

'How come you're answering the phone at my place?'

'Never mind. Listen, is this guy serious?'

There was another pause, maybe some scuffling in the background. Then Carter again. 'You'd better believe it,' he said faintly, before the kidnapper presumably ripped the phone out of his hand.

'Half a million dollars. Who has that kind of dough?' A detective asked the slow question as the opening shot in their investigation. He was thirty-something, in need of a shave, probably coming to the end of a bad day. Also, he was the solid type who rarely shows any reaction, but I guess that comes with the territory, handling homicides and hold-ups every day of your life.

'I do,' Marcie told him quietly.

The whole Carter family was sitting around their living-room, late afternoon, Wednesday. I was included in the preliminary interview, while Zig, Zoey and Connie, who had lately arrived, were expelled to the kitchen.

Sergeant Bird cast a look around at the shabby green sofa, the worn rug, as if he doubted Marcie's answer.

'She performs in a rock band,' I explained quickly, to get this slow stuff moving. 'Synergie. Have you heard them? They just made it big.'

'I guess. So this Johnny Hudson has worked out that he can screw you for half a million, no problem?' Bird didn't come across as exactly Mensa material. Like, you could practically hear the cogs in his brain whirring.

Luckily Zig's brother, Mel Wade, was also part of the investigating team. He'd asked to be put on the case because he knew the family background, and because he cared personally about what happened to Joey.

So he was the one who quickly filled his sergeant in over the old grudge between Synergie and Hudson. 'Which pinpoints the motive for the kidnap,' he explained. 'Five hundred thousand was the amount Hudson originally wanted for the copyright on what he claimed was his song. When the lawyers threw it out a year back, he wasn't a happy guy.'

Bird grunted and eased himself forward in his chair. I could see the dark stains of sweat forming across his shoulders and under his arms, coming through the pale blue shirt. 'Why wait so long?' he asked. 'Are you telling me this guy held a grudge for twelve months without taking any action? So why jump now?'

'Lately there's been another reason for Hudson to get mad, totally apart from the Synergie stuff,' Marcie told him. She glanced at me to see how uncomfortable this part made me. 'You guys down the precinct were already proceeding with an investigation into an assault by Johnny Hudson against Joey before this kidnap took place. That was to do with a fight over a girl.'

'Beth Harvey.' Mel Wade made the connection. 'Hudson had been stalking the girl after their relationship turned sour. Yeah, I see what you're saying, Marcie. By snatching Joey, Hudson enacts a two–part revenge: one, against the band and two, against the kid who stole his girl.'

'Neat,' Sergeant Bird conceded.

'Except, Beth wasn't Joey's girl any more,' I reminded the assembled audience, feeling the skin on my face tingle with embarassment. I hoped this didn't sound like sour grapes on my part.

But Mel immediately picked it up as relevant. 'Who broke it off?' he asked me, taking me to one side while Sergeant Bird plodded on with the routine questions for Mr and Mrs Carter.

I could see Mel take my answer that it was Joey who did the dumping and chew it around for a while. 'So

Joey wasn't flavour of the month with Beth Harvey any more?'

I shook my head.

'So how did Beth react?'

'I'm not sure. I don't know the girl, except seeing her from a distance once.' But I could see where Mel's thoughts were heading. 'Listen, come and talk to Connie,' I suggested. 'She has a much better idea of what was going on inside Beth Harvey's head.'

'Beth Harvey, jealous?' Connie squeaked. 'Possessive? Baby, you don't know the half of it!'

Mel and I had slipped out of the living-room into the kitchen to gain inside knowledge of the psychological make-up of Hudson's stalkee.

'Beth's the type who can't bear to share a thing, not even the air we breathe. Like, she thinks she's the Queen of England and the First Lady of America all rolled into one. A single click of her fingers, and we all have to jump to her command.'

'I guess you don't like her much?' Mel put in.

'What's to like?' Connie didn't care who knew it. 'The way she snuck in and stole Carter from under Kate's nose shows she's a selfish, scheming . . .'

'Yeah thanks, Con, we get the picture.' This time it was Zig who cut across the insults. 'But where does this get us?' he asked his big brother.

I ought to say, this was the first time Ziggy had spoken since he, Zoey and Connie had arrived. Until now he'd sat with his face screwed into a frown, quietly worried to death about his missing best buddy.

'What Connie's saying is that Beth wouldn't appreciate Carter dropping her,' I pointed out, giving Con ten out of ten for rewriting history. I mean, she left out the bit about me and Matt Kemp, making Beth's move on Carter look all the worse. 'And, what's more, even if Hudson's habit of stalking Beth was a pain in the butt, a girl like Beth might look on it as a sign that at least the guy cared!'

'Doesn't she know the difference between obsession and genuine affection?' Zoey asked mildly. Wow, could she hit the target when she wanted.

We all stared at her for a few seconds, while working our way through the maze of detail.

Carter dumps Beth. Hey, but maybe Beth never felt anything for Carter in the first place; maybe she was using him in some way – the connection between him and Synergie, for instance. She doesn't get what she wants there, so she turns against Joey.

Hadn't he told me that she didn't show up at the hospital after Hudson beat him up? So where was she during that time? Did she go out and find Hudson, instead of calling the cops and turning in her ex-boyfriend? Did she and Hudson cook up the kidnap between them? I gasped out loud as this theory mushroomed inside my head to a near-certainty.

'Share with us,' Connie invited, half-reading my mind.

'Well, the big question we're facing here isn't to do with the identity of the kidnapper. Anyone with half a brain knows that it's Hudson. But, what we need to discover is how come Carter left the house after he received the hate-mail? I mean, there's no sign of a fight, so it doesn't look like Hudson used force.'

Connie nodded. 'Someone or something persuaded him to leave of his own free will.'

'In a hurry,' I pointed out. 'Two doors were left open, no note, nothing. So, what if that someone was Beth?'

'You mean, she switched sides and hooked up with her stalker?' Mel Wade interrupted. He was having trouble with this one, obviously.

But I felt it in my bones. Beth majored in theatre studies. She could act hysterical, no problem. *Joey, Joey, horrid Hudson's after me. Please help!*

And it was all a plan, a deception, a fraud. Beth was in league with Johnny Hudson. She'd turned against Joey after he let her down in some big way. And this kidnap was her idea of revenge.

9

Fat Boys and Soft-tails, Road Kings and Sportsters; the Harleys were all lined up against the wall, gleaming yellow, red, black and silver in the dim light. Bikers' paradise.

Nightmare for me. I woke up surrounded by Evolution V-twins and Twin Cam 88Bs.

Woke up, as in came round from serious concussion, suffered when Johnny Hudson forced me up against a wall at knifepoint then crunched a brick against my skull.

Then there was a blank, ending with me regaining consciousness in some kind of semi-dark motorcycle workshop, alone except for the Fat Boys. Oh, and tied up and gagged. Groggy from the blow to the head, with a crust of dried blood caking up the left side of my face. Totally helpless actually.

I had about an hour and a half to stop feeling dizzy and for my eyes to get used to the gloom. I focused and read wall-charts about specifications such as alloy engines, Custom Chrome exhausts, crash bars and slash-cut pipes. It meant nothing to me, but it helped pass the time.

So, where was I, and why? Where were Hudson and Oscar-nominated Beth? I mean, a girl with her acting talent will go far.

The answer to my first question, so far as I could tell, was that I was in a specialist Harley Davidson repair and customising garage. I'd read ads for a place like this in my regular weekly trawl of the classified section of the local newspaper. Searching hard in my still-fuzzy memory banks, I figured that its name was Riders and it was two miles out of town on the Interstate. Not exactly the first place the cops would look for a kidnap victim.

But I saw the Johnny Hudson connection, because if my memory was accurate, the proprietor of Riders featured in the ads in absurdly giant lettering. A guy named Dave Hudson. A brother? A cousin? Father, even?

And why was I here? Because no one would come looking. You see, there was a notice pinned to the glass panel on the door to the workshop and I could read the wording in reverse. 'Closed for Summer Vacation. Re-open 1st September.' That was weeks away. Meanwhile, the dust gathered on the shiny fuel tanks and I stayed tied up.

As for the whereabouts of Johnny and Beth, I felt I'd rather remain in ignorance, thanks. I mean, I knew I'd be in serious trouble the moment they walked back into the place.

For now though, it seemed empty except for the mean machines. Although my ankles were tied and my wrists bound behind my back, I still made it to my feet by swivelling on to my knees and bunny-hopping into standing position. More bunny-hops around the greasy, oily floor showed me bits of headlamp, chrome pipe and winged Harley badges scattered everywhere.

Dave Hudson looked like a careless, messy guy to me. He didn't clean up after himself. He left out-of-date girlie calendars hanging on the walls next to bright crimson and blue graffiti sprayed from cellulose paint cans. And there were the guts of engines spread out on workbenches, worn tyres thrown into a corner – all the junk a more self-respecting customiser would've cleared out of sight.

But maybe it was junk with sharp edges that might help me cut through the rope that was tying my hands behind my back. All I needed was one jagged scrap of metal and I was on my way to freedom.

And to Kate. Kate was my main motivation for getting out of there. I mean, we'd only just come clean over how we felt, so no way was I now gonna end up with my own guts splattered over some dirty workshop floor.

So, I located my piece of metal on the workbench and

was just positioning myself to hook the rope-bracelets across the sharp edge, when a back door opened and Johnny Hudson strode in.

He was dressed in biking leathers, bareheaded, with a crazy-determined look on his face. When he saw I was attempting to escape, he rushed at me and knocked me sideways away from the bench, sending me crashing into the heap of used tyres. They softened my landing, then bounced me back towards Hudson, who grabbed me again and backed me against the wall.

'Don't even think about it!' he snarled, jamming his forearm across my throat.

My gag prevented me from answering even if I'd wanted to. So I just froze and stared at him over the top of the scummy rag that was wound around my jaw.

'You're a jerk, you know that?' Hudson's grip didn't slacken. His face was two inches from mine. I could see the saliva glisten on his teeth, the twelve-hours growth of beard on his chin. 'Only a jerk like you dumps a girl like Beth!'

I whined and shook my head; the best protest I could make.

'You don't even deserve to be the doormat under her feet; get it, jerk?'

Beth must have abandoned her intention to let the world know that she'd dumped me and gone crying to

Hudson that it was the other way around, specifically to work him up into this kind of frenzy against me. Scary stuff.

So where was Beth now? And who was in control? Was it the crazy-man stalker or the object of his desire? Of the two, Hudson or Beth, I was definitely hoping it was the girl.

I mean, crazy equals anything-can-happen. Press the wrong button and you're history. You can tell this from one look in a weirdo's eyes. You read vacant, out-to-lunch, zero contact with reality. Combined with a kitchen knife and an obsessive interest in the girl he thinks you've just dumped, the result is likely to be bad for your health.

While I came to terms with my predicament, Hudson dropped me to the floor then got busy with the telephone that was half-buried under old newspapers and unpaid bills. He dialled a number then launched into a conversation which began. 'Take a message. Listen real good . . .'

He demanded a cool half million for my release, then, before I knew it, I was talking with Kate.

'Who's that?'

'Carter, it's me, Kate.'

I should've known who it was without her telling me. I asked another dumb question by moving my sore lips and making my aching jaw work. 'How come you're answering the phone at my place?'

She ignored me and asked if Hudson was serious about the five hundred thousand dollars.

'You'd better believe it,' I answered, staring into the guy's weird eyes before he grabbed the phone and slammed it down.

'No way will they find that kind of dough,' I tried to warn him.

Major mistake: never try to reason with a psychopath. It'll send him crazy. Craz*ier*. Totally out of control.

'My folks don't have the money,' I insisted.

'Your sister's loaded, jerk. And she owes me.' Hudson strode down the row of customised Harleys lined up against the wall, ready for resale. He planned his next move out loud. 'I'll give her a couple of hours to put her hands on the dough, then make a second call identifying a drop-off point – no cops, no back-up, or her baby brother's history.' He paused near me and gave me the wild-wolf stare.

I went ahead with my sad logic. 'They'll pick you up in the end. No way will you get away with this.'

Not a smart thing for a kid with his hands and feet tied to point out to a maniac.

Hudson wheeled around and grabbed me by his favourite place: the throat. He brought out the long knife again and held its blade so that it pricked the skin under my chin.

I jerked back, so he pressed harder. The skin broke. There was a trickle of blood down my neck.

With my eyes half-shut, head jammed back against the wall, I felt the sweaty darkness of the workshop crowd in on me.

'Pray that Marcie loves you enough to part with the dough, kid.' Hudson raised the knife in front of my face. 'And hope like hell that she finds it fast.'

'How fast is fast?' I saw the knife flash, the zippers at the wrists of the crazy guy's jacket gleam dully. My breath came in short gasps; my heart beat its way through my ribs.

'Midnight,' he snarled back. 'After that, consider yourself dead.'

10

Sergeant Bird was a slow thinker, but his methods were sound.

The way he saw it, the main focus of the police investigation should be on the ransom demand. This meant sitting tight at the Carters' place, waiting for the next phone call from Hudson.

'We have all kinds of technology to put a trace on the call,' he explained to Mr and Mrs Carter. 'Once we learn where Hudson's calling from, we get our guys out there and pick him up.'

Easy. Joey's mom and dad seemed comforted by the idea, at least.

But Mel Wade put in a request to branch out. 'How about I look up Beth Harvey's address and pay a visit to her place?' he suggested. He'd taken on board the facts as Connie and I had portrayed them, thought it was worth talking with Hudson's ex-girlfriend while his sergeant played the waiting game.

Bird gave the OK.

'Want to take a ride in the car with me, girls?' Mel

dropped in the idea that Connie and I should go along to help him identify Beth when he paid the official visit.

So we drove from Marytown over to East Village, siren blasting, forcing the traffic to pull over as we zoomed through. This was better than sitting around watching Marcie and the rest go quietly crazy over Joey; the speed and action gave me the illusion that we were making some progress.

Hitting Franklin Avenue, Mel killed the siren and the blue light and began to cruise more steadily towards Beth Harvey's apartment block. We arrived low-key, sliding into a parking bay by the main entrance and stepping quickly inside the building. Mel waved his badge at the guy on the door, who then directed us via the main elevator to the tenth floor and Beth's place.

So far, everything had gone without a hitch, and both Con and I were picturing a rapid resolution in the shape of a tough interrogation by Mel, followed by a guilty disintegration on the part of Beth, leading to the exact location of the crazy kidnapper and imminent arrest. Oh, and then the part where I fall into Carter's arms. Don't forget that.

Only one problem: when Mel pushed Beth's doorbell there was no reply.

A door on the landing two storeys down from us

opened instead and a red-haired woman poked her nose into our business.

'You looking for Beth Harvey?' she yelled up the stairwell.

There were two unusual aspects to this. One, that the neighbour knew the name of another resident in the block. Two, that she cared who came knocking on doors. I mean, this was a typical, anonymous tower block where nameless people went about their daily grind.

The woman with the flame-coloured hair came labouring up the stairs to join us. She was creased and crumpled, with smudged pink lips, wearing rubber flip-flops that smacked against the stone steps. 'Try again,' she suggested to Mel, with a brief, faded smile at Connie and me. 'I know she's in there.'

'You do?' Mel pressed the buzzer a second time.

'Sure. She had a visitor a couple of hours back, and I know for sure she didn't leave since then.'

Despite this, the door stayed stubbornly shut.

'How come you know so much about your neighbour's movements?' Mel quizzed the woman.

'Because she always enters and leaves by the fire escape, and it passes right by my window. That's how come I noticed the kid getting beaten up in the alleyway a couple of days back.'

'You're the lady who got Joey Carter to the hospital?' I asked, thanking the Lord for nosy neighbours.

'That was me,' she confirmed proudly. 'And I'm telling you, you need to try harder to get an answer now. I mean, I didn't exactly like what I heard when that guy in the leather suit came calling.'

Mel heard enough to put in a request to his officer-in-charge for permission to enter the apartment without a search warrant.

'The neighbour heard some kind of fight. She says there was a lot of noise, then Hudson came hurtling down the fire escape. She spent the last two hours wondering whether to call us, then I showed up and solved her problem.'

Sergeant Bird said for Mel to go ahead and report right back.

'Oh Jeez, why did I wait?' the woman sighed as she watched Mel use his shoulder against the lock. No good; the door stayed in place. 'Hey, come through my apartment and up the fire escape, why don't you?'

So we followed her, overtaking her in her living-room and taking the metal staircase two steps at a time. We found the glass-panelled door to Beth's apartment splintered into a thousand fragments and a scene of chaos like you'd never believe.

The shattered glass lay over the floor amidst upturned tables and chairs, a spilt flower vase, scattered magazines. The white drape which had hung across one window had been torn down and dragged across the rug; an inner door had been wrenched off its hinges.

'Oh my God!' the neighbour gasped, arriving out of breath long after we'd taken in the mess. 'What happened?'

'Don't move. Don't touch a thing,' Mel warned us, picking his way beyond the torn drape and through the broken door.

'This is down to Hudson!' Connie breathed. 'He wrecked the whole place!'

I felt a shiver down my spine in that muggy, airless room. 'What can you see?' I called to Mel, who by this time had disappeared into Beth's small bathroom.

He came back out shaking his head. 'Someone lost a lot of blood in there,' he said quietly.

Which was when I picked up a dark trail across the rug, leading to the heap of ripped fabric behind the sofa. Without stopping to think, I rushed forward, grabbed a corner of the drape and pulled it to one side.

Underneath there was a body slumped on its stomach, the head turned sideways at an awkward angle, a trail of blood trickling from its open mouth.

'I got a pulse!' Mel yelled. He went into emergency resuscitation mode, checking Beth Harvey's airway and beginning to administer the kiss of life.

Connie called the ambulance, while Beth's remorseful, asthmatic neighbour collapsed out on the landing. My head was spinning. What could I do? Yeah, drag the torn drape out of Mel's way so he could turn the unconscious body on to its back and do the mouth-to-mouth.

I tried not to look at Beth's face as Mel changed her position again. Even so, I caught the deadly white skin and the crimson trickle.

'She has blood in her oesophagus, maybe in her lungs as well.' Mel had listened to the victim's rattling, broken breath by leaning his ear against Beth's thorax. 'Kate, help me get her back on to her side, into the recovery position. It looks like she can breathe unaided, but lack of oxygen has put her into a coma. We need the paramedics to get here fast!'

Moving her gently, wiping away the blood from her face and chest, I noticed for the first time a gaping wound. It ran from the base of her throat diagonally down towards her armpit, about five inches long and very deep.

This is where the drape came in useful. There

was blood still leaking from the cut which had to be stopped. So I tore a strip and made a pad of fabric, then pressed it against the wound to stem the flow.

'Good work,' Mel told me. 'The question is, did she already lose too much before we got here?'

Only the experts could tell us this, we knew. The wait for the ambulance to arrive seemed to last an age. Time stretched, then telescoped as soon as we picked up the wail of the siren. After that, the paramedics coming on the scene with the stretcher, the oxygen mask, the decision to intubate all seemed to roll into ten action-packed seconds.

'Will she be OK?' the frightened neighbour asked over and over as the two medics carried the loaded stretcher along the corridor.

'Stand out of the way, lady, please!' one ordered without providing any answers. 'We need to get this patient down to ER and into theatre fast!'

Mel Wade drove with Connie and me on the tail of the ambulance through the evening streets.

Once more, the slow traffic parted at the sound of the sirens, drivers glancing out of their windows to wonder in passing, 'Why the police escort? Which poor sucker got himself shot, stabbed or mugged this time? And in broad daylight too.'

And during the drive to Fortune City General, Mel was in constant contact with Sergeant Bird.

'We got a major development,' he reported. 'Our chief suspect seems to have forced entry into Beth Harvey's apartment, wrecked the joint and stabbed its occupant.'

This produced silence from the sergeant. Enough of a gap for me to picture the way Hudson must have turned against Beth, flung wild accusations at her, flipped and got out the knife.

'How's the victim?' Bird asked eventually.

'Alive but in a coma.'

'OK, stick with her. Wait at the hospital to see if you can gather anything new. Now that this thing's hotting up, I'll put out a search for Hudson in all his usual haunts.'

'How's it going at your end?' Mel asked, skirting wide of a truck that half-blocked the entrance to the hospital. As he pulled up by the main entrance to the ER, Connie and I jumped out of the car.

'Nothing new here. We have Marcie sitting by the phone, still waiting for Hudson to get in touch.'

'What's the plan? Are you gonna convince him that she'll show up with the five hundred thousand?'

'Yeah. She knows to keep him talking while we get a fix on his position.'

Mel listened and considered things. 'Listen, Greg, you go easy, OK?'

'Sure. We won't jump unless we know we can get the Carter kid out in one piece. Is that what you're saying?'

'The Carter kid.' Joey. Personally, I didn't care about the dollars. Only about him. The tension of the situation got to me so bad that I found it difficult to breathe.

'Easy,' Connie murmured. 'C'mon, Kate, this is gonna work out, you'll see.'

Mel signed off from his radio conversation and followed us into the hospital, where we discovered that events had continued to move fast.

'The patient's in surgery.' One of the paramedics from the scene came across the lobby to keep us informed. 'We started a transfusion while she was in the ambulance. It looks like there's some damage to an artery in the neck which they need to repair, and possible damage to organs due to loss of blood.'

'What are her chances?' Mel wanted to know.

The bright lights, the trolleys, the phones ringing, the monitors and nurses rushing by all got to me as the paramedic delivered his opinion by way of a non-committal shrug. 'I guess all we can do is wait and see.'

Wait, while Beth Harvey's life hung on a thread and

the crazy guy who stabbed her was currently holding Carter for ransom. *Yeah, you try waiting patiently in these circumstances*, I thought.

'Which one of you is Kate Brennan?' A nurse came out of the Intensive Treatment Unit one hour after Beth had been wheeled in for surgery.

I stood up on shaky legs. 'That's me.'

'The patient just regained consciousness,' the nurse reported. 'She wants to speak with you.'

Glancing at Mel, who nodded and got ready to accompany me, I followed the nurse across the white tiled floor. 'Why me?' I wanted to know.

The nurse – a young woman with a mass of dark curls tied back and hidden beneath a surgical cap – told us that all she knew was that Beth had asked to see me urgently.

'This is good!' Mel reassured me in a low voice. 'It means she trusts you and has something she wants to tell you.'

So we went ahead through swing-doors into a cubicle containing a bed backed by a bank of monitors and metal stands for plasma and saline fluid. Tubes were looped and draped on to the bed, attached to the patient who lay absolutely still beneath a pale blue sheet.

I hesitated and glanced at the nurse.

'Go ahead.' She gestured me into position beside the bed.

Beth lay with her eyes closed, a white dressing hiding the horrific knife wound across her chest. Sensing my approach, she turned her head and opened her eyes. She spoke her first word. 'Sorry.'

'What for?' I leaned over and listened hard.

'For Carter,' she whispered. 'I told Johnny not to hurt him. I said, no way would I stay involved if he used violence.'

I nodded then glanced at Mel who stood to one side listening. 'Get the location!' he mouthed slowly.

'You knew about the kidnapping?' I asked Beth.

'Sorry!' she breathed, tears forming and beginning to roll down her cheeks. 'I was mad at Carter and his sister. I had this stupid idea that I could use Johnny to get back at them. Only, I overlooked the fact that the guy's crazy!'

'So he got out of control and you had a fight?' I prompted. 'He tried to kill you?'

Beth sighed and nodded. 'Johnny told me he planned to pick up the money but not hand Joey over. His idea was to kill him anyway, dump the body in a gas station restroom, then pick up the dough and ride his Harley north over the Canadian border. He said finishing off the kid before he did the deal would be a final twist of the knife.'

'Which gas station?' I asked, seizing my chance. 'C'mon, Beth, better still: where is Hudson holding Carter prisoner?'

She blinked the tears out of her eyes and looked right at me. 'At a place called Riders. It's a motorcycle workshop belonging to Johnny's cousin, out on the Interstate.' She paused, then came out with an urgent question. 'Kate, what time is it now?'

Mel held up his wristwatch for me to read. 'Eleven-thirty,' I told Beth. 'Why?'

'You gotta move fast,' she gasped. 'Johnny's plan was to wait until midnight, do the deed and then head north on the Harley.'

11

'You bring the dough to the gas station on the Interstate, two miles out of town, heading north,' Hudson instructed Marcie down the phone. 'Midnight. No tricks, no funny business, OK?'

He pressed a button so I could hear her answer.

'Midnight at the gas station,' she confirmed.

'You stash the used bills in a black garbage sack and dump it in the telephone kiosk outside the restrooms. I'll be around to watch you do it, but you won't know I'm there.'

Midnight was under an hour away. Less than sixty minutes until I got out of this mess. I hoped. The cords were cutting deep into my wrists and ankles, I felt stifled by the dirty piece of rag tied round my mouth.

'How do we know that you're keeping your side of the deal?' Marcie wanted to know. 'You have to bring Joey to the spot, or else I won't drop the dough.'

Hudson laughed. 'Yeah, right!'

'I'm serious! You bring my brother, I leave the five hundred thousand. Otherwise, no deal.'

Don't push your luck, Marcie! I watched Hudson's face darken as my sister began to call some of the shots. 'Listen, honey. Trust me, OK? If I promise to set Joey free as part of the negotiation, you just have to believe me. Think about it.'

He was pointing out the lack of choice in the situation, getting edgier by the second. He flung me a look of pure hatred as I lay curled up amongst the used tyres, like it was down to *me* that Marcie was being difficult.

At last, after a gap of several seconds, she came through. 'OK, I'll do it your way. The money will be in the kiosk dead on midnight. So where do I find Joey?'

'You wait until I've picked up the dough, leave it until I'm out of sight, then look for him in the last cubicle to the right in the men's restroom,' Hudson instructed. 'Your brother's here listening to this conversation. Is there anything you want to say to him?'

I shivered under the rubber mountain. Why did this sound like giving the condemned man his last request?

'Joey, hold on. I'll get you out of there, believe me.' Marcie did a good job of sounding confident, but couldn't quite disguise the tremble in her voice.

'Sweet!' Hudson sneered. Then to Marcie, 'I'm afraid he can't come to the phone; he's tied up right now.'

He slammed down the phone on what he thought was a witticism, but which fell pretty flat with me.

The fact was, Hudson was pleased with himself. He got busy now, checking the fuel level in the tank of his Harley, opening up the workshop door so that I could see out into a dark, empty yard surrounded by a high razor-wire fence. And he was in talkative mood, the way some normally introspective guys get when things go well for them.

The only problem was, the information he was giving me was stuff he'd never admit to if he planned to keep me alive. Like, it was incriminatory as hell, and made me freak out big time.

'So, Joey,' he said, real friendly, as he eased his motorcycle towards the door. Some distance away, a heavy truck rolled by on the Interstate. 'That's one loyal sister you have out there. Yeah, it kinda sucks to disappoint her, but that's what I'm gonna have to do.'

Hudson clicked the ignition and turned over the engine of his gleaming machine, opening the throttle, then letting it idle on its stand as he came back to deal with me.

'Problem is, a guy gets himself in too deep,' he explained. 'And once you're in the way I am, there's no turning back, see?'

If this sounds like a friendly approach, forget it. Menace is what we're talking: the way Hudson strolled over in his leathers and took his kitchen knife from the bench, then stooped over me to admit the difficulty he faced.

'You get blood over your hands once, twice, three times; what's the difference? They can only put you in jail for one lifetime. The way I figure it is, what I did to Beth I can do again. I mean, I felt a lot for that girl; don't get me wrong. She was the most beautiful thing; those green eyes, that mouth . . .'

While Hudson reminisced, I shivered some more and squirmed to get up on my feet. The guy's use of the past tense in referring to Beth was chilling.

'Yeah, and I thought for a while there that Beth and me could get it back together. She was into this kidnap deal for a while, but it turned out she didn't have the guts to go through with it. This made her freak out, see?'

When he said 'this', Hudson jerked the point of the knife at my chest.

I was on my knees, struggling to stand up, but then I froze.

'Pity,' he went on. 'Beth's problem was, she came on too heavy, like starting to yell and scream in the bathroom when I tried to convince her we had to go the whole way with this deal – no fooling around, no leaving you free to talk to the cops. I mean, it was clear to me from the start that no way would you be able to walk out of this.'

Jesus; he'd stabbed his girlfriend, and now he was gonna stab me. With the knife digging into my ribs, I'd never been more sure of anything in my life.

I did the drowning-man bit; saw my life flash before my eyes – my mom and dad, Marcie, Damien and Fern, all staring at me with sad eyes. Me leaping up and shooting a ball into the net. Kate floating towards me in a dreamy manner, saying, 'Yeah, Carter, I always loved you . . .'

Out on the highway, a vehicle drove off the carriageway and cruised around the back lots towards the Riders yard. Its headlights raked across the dark trading estate, illuminating brick walls and the razor-wire fence.

'You guys are so naive,' Hudson sneered. The visitor's headlights had worried him a little, but not enough to distract him from his task. 'You think that if a guy gives you his word, that counts for something. I mean, picture your sister's face when she opens the door to that restroom and finds you in not quite the condition she'd hoped for . . .'

I held my breath, felt the pressure of the knifepoint increase against my ribs.

Then the car outside stopped, its lights beaming straight into the workshop yard.

Hudson registered it, pressed harder with the knife, then spun round, tucked the knife into his belt and jumped up to deal with the interruption.

I breathed out hard and slumped forward, watched him race for the open doorway.

Then I was up and shuffling towards the bench, scrabbling for that piece of sharp metal which I'd located earlier. Jamming it into an upright position, I turned my back, hoisted my wrists and hooked the rope over its edge. I chafed it like crazy, rubbing until the cord snapped.

Outside the yard, the unsuspecting car driver dimmed his headlights, leaving Hudson standing in the dark. He yelled for the unwanted visitor to turn round and drive the hell away, no doubt imagining some quiet romantic interlude about to take place between the driver and female passenger in the steamed-up auto.

This all happened fast; just enough time for me to cut through the rope that tied my wrists, then grab the metal fragment and work on my ankles. When the second rope snapped, I knew that at least I stood a chance against the maniac with the knife.

Luckily, the driver didn't like being yelled at. He got out of the car to argue, keeping Hudson busy while I got used to my arms and legs being free and giving me the time to rip the gag away from my mouth.

But only just. By now, Hudson had backed off from the loving couple in disgust and was in the process of sliding the workshop door closed so he could come back and deal with me in private. When he saw I was free, he swore, took out his knife and made a run towards me between two bikes in the row.

Five seconds and that knife would slice between my ribs. So? I judged the distance between me and the slit in the half-closed sliding-door. I saw Hudson's Harley idling quietly nearby, gave myself a fifty-fifty chance of reaching it before he did.

Then I vaulted the bench and made a run for the bike. I leaped into the saddle of a machine I'd never ridden in my life before. Jeez, I had like two seconds to learn.

Hudson crashed into one of the parked bikes and sent it toppling into another. The row fell like dominoes with a scrape and crunch of crumpling metal.

I opened the throttle and made the engine roar, felt the machine jerk forward, released the brake and shot out through the narrow gap into the yard.

Behind me, I heard Hudson pick up a second machine and urge it into life. Me in front, squealing across the yard on the back wheel; him behind, about to catch me and slam me against the wall.

Death at knifepoint or by crushing? That was the stark choice.

And by now, Hudson didn't care that there were witnesses: three, not two people stepping out of the parked Ford, all running towards us and me recognising the guy first.

'Joey, over here!' Mel Wade yelled and waved at me to head across the yard towards the gate he was opening.

I came down on to two wheels, regained control and swung round away from the wall. But could I steer the machine through the gate before Hudson rammed into me? His bike was a monster, big and heavy. Mine was lighter, faster.

Mel pulled the gate open and stood back beside Kate and Connie.

My mind took them in with a fleeting glance. No time to ask myself questions like, how come they were here? Instead, I swerved by, wrenching at the handlebars to avoid their car and finding myself flying across a stretch of rough, brick-strewn ground. I hit a bump and bounced out of the saddle, hearing Hudson still close behind. I landed with a thump that jarred my whole body, steadied the bike then rode on.

Ahead of me was a patch of broken concrete about twenty yards square, beyond that, another hardly noticeable ten-foot barrier of razor-wire, with low buildings to either side. Dead end.

My heart jumped into my mouth as I shot forward on to the concrete surface, with Hudson so close behind I could feel him almost touch my back wheel. The two bikes whined and screamed. I felt the smooth surface under the wheels, left it until the last split second to brake and U-turn away from the razor-wire.

Too fast for Hudson, who didn't see the fence until he

rode right into it.

The barrier snared him and brought him crashing down. The wire cut right through his leather jacket and left him hooked, arms spread wide in crucifixion pose, body broken, while the bike he was riding skidded from under him.

By the time I braked and brought my own bike to a halt, Mel Wade, Connie and Kate had all reached the spot. We ran together to where Johnny Hudson was hanging.

'Don't touch him!' Mel warned.

I wasn't about to. Something in the way his head hung down, eyes open but not looking at us, told me he was already dead.

THE KISS 1

Lots of stuff left me confused – like the way Mel had abandoned his squad car and commandeered a plain Ford in order for him, Kate and Connie to creep up on Hudson's hiding-place. Like Beth confessing the location to Kate and them arriving ahead of Sergeant Bird and a whole convoy of police vehicles. Like a medic arriving on the scene to confirm that Hudson had broken his neck and cut his jugular by riding into the razor-wire barrier at speed. They carried him off in a body bag with no one to lament his passing, except, later, Beth who said she would always blame herself for winding him up to kidnap me in the first place. The cops interpreted this as Beth liking to hold centre-stage and gently sent her home. Lucky Beth.

All this was fuzzy then, but became clear later.

I do remember vividly the reunion down the precinct with Mom, Dad and the rest of the family. Tears of relief, chastisements, hugs, kisses. *Never ever do this to us again!*

'Joey, promise me, you won't look at another Harley as long as you live!' This was Dad coming on strong, fixing on the one point I'd hoped he would overlook. I mean, I'd conquered that dream-machine in seconds. I'd even outridden an expert!

And, to be honest, somewhere in my mind I still harbour the dream of riding west into the sunset on a gleaming Harley Davidson.

With Kate riding pillion.

We got our kiss in the end, though we had to store it up until we could be private. I mean, you can't get up-close and personal with your kid brother hanging on to your shirt.

So it was Thursday, and the cops were off our backs; investigation closed. Most things were back to normal.

Except my lip, which was still a touch swollen from Hudson's previous beating.

Kate and I were alone, chilling out in the basement at my place, playing tracks from Marcie's latest CD.

'Does that hurt?' she asked, reaching out to feel the sore place with her fingertips.

'Uh-huh,' I grunted. *Tingle, tingle. Electric touch*. I leaned towards her to prove my point.

Our lips met. Soft. My eyes were open and I could see the fuzzy outline of Kate's smiling mouth, nose and dark eyelashes.

This was a dream. No – this was really happening. At last.

THE KISS 2

Weird things happen. The person I hugged when Hudson rode into the barrier was Connie. We held each other and turned our eyes away, gave thanks that it wasn't Carter tangled up in that razor-wire.

Connie and I will be friends forever, I guess.

But it was Carter I wanted to take in my arms.

Not yet though.

There was family, cops, paramedics, a corpse to deal with.

Then, next day, time to ourselves in Joey's basement.

I'd watched him turn down the volume to Synergie's music, saw him sit next to me, close enough to reach out and touch.

We were both nervous, in spite of what we'd almost confessed on the phone. Like, this was still a major move.

'Does that hurt?' I whispered, leaning forward to stroke his lip.

The answer came in a kiss. Lips together, grinning like crazy.

                    *   *   *

And was it worth the wait?

That was yesterday, and I'm still smiling, believe
me.